wonderland

I don't know what's wrong with me today – I've been infected by the impetuous bug (or I've just gone mad finally). First I go out and get my eyebrow stapled after thinking about it for all of 0.5 seconds, and now I'm scrabbling about in a stupidly messy drawer for the old red address book that I know contains a phone number that I've never tried, and that Helen has only used in emergencies, like when the paternity payment hasn't come through on time.

Omigod. I'm about to call my father. I'd better do it quick before the sane part of me susses out what I'm up to…

wonderland

KAREN McCOMBIE

SCHOLASTIC

For Trisha McCombie, with loads of love

First published in the UK in 2002 by Scholastic Children's Books
An imprint of Scholastic Ltd
Euston House, 24 Eversholt Street
London, NW1 1DB, UK
Registered office: Westfield Road,
Southam, Warwickshire, CV47 0RA
SCHOLASTIC and associated logos are trademarks and or
registered trademarks of Scholastic Inc.

This edition published by Scholastic Ltd, 2007

Text copyright © Karen McCombie, 2002
The right of Karen McCombie to be identified as the author of this work has
been asserted by her.

10 digit ISBN 0 439 94297 7
13 digit ISBN 978 0439 94297 3

British Library Cataloguing-in-Publication Data.
A CIP catalogue record for this book is available from the British Library

Printed and bound in Great Britain by Bookmarque Ltd, Croydon
Papers used by Scholastic Children's Books are made from wood grown in
sustainable forests.

3 5 7 9 10 8 6 4 2

This is a work of fiction. Names, characters, places, incidents and dialogues are
products of the author's imagination or are used fictitiously. Any resemblance to
actual people, living or dead, events or locales is entirely coincidental.

www.scholastic.co.uk/zone

chapter one

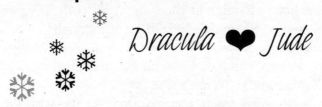

Dracula ❤ *Jude*

Date:	*Thursday 31st October*
Stressometer rating: ❄	*Low. But may get higher if Shaunna keeps winding me up*
Wish of the moment: ❄	*That I find true love. (The same wish I wish the other 364 days of the year...)*

"Dracula fancies you."

I glance over in Dracula's direction – he's standing under a banner that says "Happy 18th Birthday, Josh!" with Gladiator and Harry Potter. OK, so he's looking over in our direction, but so what?

"He does *not* fancy me!" I tell my friend.

Shaunna – what's she like? She's already been saying that the Viking, the Cossack, Frodo Baggins and Postman Pat have all been eyeing me up. I mean, yeah, so I *have* danced with the Viking and the Cossack, and I *did* get chatting to Frodo Baggins in the queue for the coat room, but honestly, that hardly means they're all desperate to go out with me or anything…

"Your wig's tilting," says Molly, walking over to join us and immediately hauling at the long, dark, curly, permed frizz perched on Shaunna's head till it sits straight.

"Thank you. So's yours," Shaunna replies, giving Molly's very blonde, very *real* hair a playful tug in return.

"Ow!" grins Molly. "What's that for?"

"For disappearing for so long! Nobody knows who I'm supposed to be when I'm on my own! We only work when we're together!"

Shaunna's right – standing side by side in their matching satin trousers, '70s puff-sleeved blouses (in naff nylon) and luminous blue eyeshadow, it's easy to see that Molly and Shaunna have come to the fancy dress party tonight as the girls out of ABBA. But on her own, Shaunna does tend to look like she's just turned up as someone with exceptionally bad taste in clothes, wearing the sort of cheap and tacky wig you can order out of the small ads at the back of newspapers. (Actually, she got hers in a charity shop on the high street. She had to wash it before she could wear it – it looked like a gerbil had been using it to give birth in.)

"I've been through watching Dean and Adam play pool," Molly tells us, throwing her thumb over her chiffon-y shoulder in the direction of the bar area, just off the main function suite.

"Must have been fascinating." I fake a yawn. I like both my friends' boyfriends very much, but the idea of hovering round a table while they poke at tiny balls with sticks seems like a waste of good party time to me.

"Well, it *was* pretty funny, when you consider what they're wearing." Molly grins, and *then* I get it. Dean's come as a boxer tonight, complete with big, padded red gloves which he's so far refused to take off (he's been drinking his beer through a straw) and Adam – being Adam – has come as a sumo wrestler, all zipped up into one of those giant fat suits. I guess the fact that one player can't hold his pool stick and the other player probably can't even get *near* the pool table *would* make the game kind of interesting.

"Anyway, you've been missing all the fun, Mol!"

Uh-oh – Shaunna has one of those wicked looks on her face.

"Yeah, what's been happening?" Molly glances at both of us.

"All the boys are drooling over our goth witch buddy, here."

"They are not!" I squeak.

"Oh, stop being so coy, Jude," Shaunna teases me with a smile. "You look gorgeous tonight, so why shouldn't they drool over you?"

Do witches blush? Probably not – but I do, in an all too human way. I'm not too hot at taking compliments, if you want to know the truth. I never know what to say in return, specially if it's a boy who's doling them out. Coming out with "thank you" sounds a bit berky and smug to me, so with boys I usually end up just snogging them (I know – bad, isn't it?), or turning it into a joke. Like now.

"I cast a spell over Shaunna," I shrug at Molly. "A spell where she only says nice things to me."

"But you *do* look great!" says Molly. "Specially with that ivy in your hair!"

Ah, the ivy. Nicked, by my own fair hand, from Westburn Park earlier today. I got the idea for that from these two art nouveau posters that Helen – my mum – has hanging on her bedroom walls. I think it must have been the law back in the late 1800s that all women had to pose for paintings with shrubberies entangled in their hair. Whatever, it helped give me a bit of inspiration, 'cause when I first tried on Helen's long black dress, all I looked like was ... me in a long black dress. Not a particularly stunning get-up for a fancy dress party ("And first prize goes to Jude, for coming as... Jude!"). It was my short, spiky dark hair; *that* was what was spoiling the witch effect I'd planned. Even after I added black, fingerless lace gloves, ghostly pale foundation and blood red lips, the witch thing *still* wasn't coming together. I did toy with buying a pointy hat out of the toy shop in the precinct, but they'd sold out, since it's Halloween and every kid in town had snapped them up already. But then last night I went into Helen's room (to steal my hairdryer back from my light-fingered mother) and found myself gawping at those languid ladies on the posters. Next thing, it was a case of – ping! – problem solved. If you'd have come looking for me around teatime today, you'd have found me in the kitchen, coming over all *Blue Peter* and doing creative things with wire coat hangers and plant life. And here's one I made earlier: a gothic bridesmaid's floral circlet of ivy and dripping red berries. (Don't ask me to get technical and tell you what kind of berries they are. They're the pretty kind, OK?)

"So anyway, Mrs Coy here is pretending not to notice that half the guys in here fancy her!" Shaunna winds me up by saying. "And she *still* doesn't seem interested in any of them."

"I was!" I insist. "I thought the Viking was quite cute ...

till he nearly took my eye out with one of his horns when we were dancing to Nirvana –"

Lesson 1: If you're going to go to a fancy dress party as a Viking, *don't* do any head-banging while wearing your helmet; you could seriously injure your fellow dancers.

"– and I quite liked the Cossack, till he showed me up."

Lesson 2: If you're going to a fancy dress party as a Cossack, don't feel you *have* to get down on your haunches and give a demonstration of authentic Cossack dancing. For a start, it won't be authentic (specially not when you're doing it to a Craig David track), and for another thing, you'll probably fall over (specially if you've been drinking beer) and will look like a total muppet. And so will your dance partner.

"What about Frodo, then? He's sweet!"

Ah, Frodo. Shaunna's right – he *is* sweet, but…

"Look, I don't mean to be mean here," I wince, "but sweet or not, that guy is *actual* Hobbit-sized."

It's true. I'm pretty tall, so if by some quirk of fate me and Frodo *did* fall for each other, the only way I'd be able to comfortably snog him in an upright position is if I stood in a ditch.

"Well, that leaves Postman Pat and Dracula, then. What about Pat? If you ask nicely, maybe he'll show you his black and white cat!"

Postman Pat is Josh – whose birthday party this is – and he's a friend of Dean's. He's cute, but *bunny* cute, if you see what I mean. It's like, who would dress as a dorky kids' TV character for their own birthday party? Wouldn't you want to come as someone cool or dynamic, like Zorro, or Liam Gallagher or Bart Simpson even? And that's my trouble: I never go for the cute, sweet, nice guys, whether they're dressed as Postman Pat or not. (Molly set me up with a nice guy she knew only last month, and our date was nice ... and absolutely *nothing* else.)

I try, I *really* do try, but I have this fatal flaw ... boys with the middle name "Trouble" get me every time. If there's a charming rat out there, I'll fall for him. If there's a double-crossing, two-timing scumbag around, I'll melt at the first smile he beams my way. It's not healthy, and I don't like it. In fact, I'd give anything to be 1000% in love like Shaunna and Adam are, like Molly and Dean are, but I just don't know how to de-sensitize the bad-lad magnet lodged in my heart...

"So that means we're down to Dracula," Shaunna muses. "Hmm, he'd be pretty good-looking without those fangs..."

"Which Dracula are we talking about? I've seen three tonight so far."

"Over by the banner, Molly," I whisper quickly, before Shaunna gets a chance to bellow it out loud.

"Oh, God – not *him*, Jude!" Molly looks at me in alarm after checking out "my" Dracula. "Josh's sister was just telling me about him—"

"Which one is Josh's sister?" Shaunna can't help but interrupt.

"The one dressed as Britney Spears."

Shaunna and I both wince, thinking exactly the same thing. And then Shaunna puts it into words.

"If *I* was her, I think I'd have waited till my belly-ring piercing stopped being infected before I flashed my stomach around!"

"Whatever," Molly says, mildly impatiently, as she tries to get on with what she was talking about. "She told me that Dracula over there nearly got expelled from his school at the start of this term for riding his Vespa over the school lawn and ripping it to shreds."

Uh-oh. He's trouble.

"And his last girlfriend threatened to take pills when he dumped her, but he never even went to *see* her when he heard."

A heartless heartbreaker. Tsk, tsk, tsk.

"Oh, yeah – he's a total big-head, apparently. He thinks every girl should fall at his feet. A couple of weeks ago, he started chatting Josh's sister up, but she knocked him back. And she says he's such a git that he's ignored her all night tonight, just 'cause of that."

"He's probably ignoring her 'cause he can't bear the sight of her septic, yellow belly button..." Shaunna smirks.

But I notice Molly isn't smirking. She's just glanced over in the direction of Dracula and is now turning her ashen face back to us.

"Omigod, don't look now ... but Dracula's on his way over!" she hisses through clenched teeth.

He's a big-headed, troublemaking, heartless heartbreaker, I mumble to myself, slightly alarmed at how excited I suddenly feel.

"Well, let's start talking about something else, quick!" Shaunna suggests. "Who was winning at pool when you left, Molly?"

"No one. Dean had shot the white ball off the table and they were both scrabbling around on their hands and knees looking for it."

Or on their stomach, in Adam-the-sumo-wrestler's case.

While my friends flip effortlessly to this cover-up conversation, I sense the approach of Dracula (a swish of black cape out of the corner of my eye) and feel my heart try and pickaxe its way out of my chest. Of course it might not be me he likes. It could be Shaunna. (Erm, in *that* wig?!)

He's a big-headed, troublemaking, heartless heartbreaker, I repeat to myself. *And I must not touch him with a bargepole. He's a big-headed, troublemaking—*

"Hi. Sorry to interrupt…"

It's Dracula, smiling a killer smile at us all, but letting it settle on me. Uh-oh.

He's a big-headed, troublemaking, heartbreakingly gorgeous love god…

"…but I just wondered if the beautiful witch fancied a dance?"

Help.

The big-headed, troublemaking, heartless heartbreaker is called Mitchell. Mitchell McKenzie. I think it makes him sound like a male supermodel. John Galliano and Stella McCartney would fight over which one of them gets him for their next Milan catwalk show. *Elle* magazine will feature Mitchell McKenzie as the next bright young thing, and in their feature, there'll be jaw-droppingly great photos of him, and a touching interview where he credits his ever-loving girlfriend Jude Conrad for keeping him grounded through all his success. Jude, a fellow model-cum-actress—

"Hey, what are you doing after this?" I hear Mitchell

McKenzie mutter as he breaks away from me.

What does he mean? After we stop kissing? Or after the party finishes? I'm momentarily disorientated, what with being lost in snogsville there...

"After this?" I repeat, dumbly, playing for time till my brain flips from daydreams to reality.

Me and Mitchell McKenzie have spent the last hour together, dancing and getting to know one another. Oh, and snogging. I know, I know, I *know* I shouldn't have (I can tell from the occasional frosty looks I catch from Shaunna and Molly that they think I *definitely* shouldn't have), but there're two sides to every story, aren't there? Isn't that true? It's like the business with Mitchell nearly getting expelled; he told me all about it, how he flipped and drove his scooter over the school lawns, because this one bully of a teacher had pushed him to the edge, hassling him over his A levels. And that ex-girlfriend of his? The pill-popper? She was a major fruitcake who he wasn't even properly going out with. And as for Josh's sister: it's not just her belly button that's poisonous – apparently, it was her who came on to *him*, and when he knocked *her* back, she started bad-mouthing him to anyone who'd listen. Like Molly tonight.

"I mean, what are you doing after the party," Mitchell mumbles, throwing his cloak back off his wrist and checking his watch. "It's nearly 12 now – they'll be chucking us all out soon."

"I was just going to get a cab home with my friend Shaunna – she lives across the road from me."

"Well, what if I jump in the cab with you?" he grins, looking for a split-second like Jack Nicholson as The Joker in the *Batman* movies. "You said your mum wouldn't be back till late…"

It's like I can see the dot, dot, dot trailing off at the end of his sentence, and I know *exactly* what he's implying. And if I hadn't been sure, I think the fact that he's now rubbing his *groin* against me is a bit of a giveaway. God, I only mentioned that Helen would be late home tonight because she's at the same gig at the university union that Mitchell's brother's gone to.

"So?" he smiles wickedly at me, and for a moment there I think he's still got his plastic fangs in. "How about it, Jade?"

All of a sudden, the music grinds to an ungainly halt, someone flips the main lights on and somewhere outside I hear church bells start clanging out midnight chimes. Maybe I've got *both* my pointy, black shoes wedged safely on my feet, but apart from that, I think I'm having a Cinderella moment…

Forget the handsome, misunderstood guy sweeping me off my feet; without my fairytale glasses on, I can see him for what he really is – a creep on the pull, with his winking cronies standing leering and laughing at us on the side, wondering how lucky their mate's going to get tonight. Well, he was never, *ever* going to get *that* lucky, but now that he can't even be bothered getting my name right, I don't think he deserves one more microsecond of my time.

"Oi, Jade! Where are you going?" I hear him call after me as soon as I've speed-walked away from him, wiping his kisses from my mouth with the back of my hand.

Ignoring him, I stride across the room to the two girly members of ABBA, who are frowning at me, looking as puzzled as Dracula did when I left him behind without a word.

"That's *it*!" I tell my friends, yanking my ivy headdress off and tossing it in the nearest bin. "I've finally *had* it with low-life losers…"

Shaunna and Molly exchange looks that say "Yeah, *right*!"

"No, honestly! I have!" I try to mumble as Molly takes a paper tissue out of her pocket and starts rubbing smeared red lipstick off my face. (I tell you, she's more mumsy towards me than Helen ever is.)

"Jude, if you've finished with bad lads," Shaunna giggles, "then I'm a Teletubby."

"OK, so which one are you?" I ask her. "Laa-Laa or Tinky Winky?"

And then my world goes dark, as a gerbil-scented wig gets splatted on my head and tugged low down over my face.

But you know something? Whatever Shaunna and Molly think, I'm going to prove them wrong. Call it a New Year's Resolution. (It's only two months early…)

chapter two

Officially bored

Date: *Saturday 2nd November*

Stressometer rating: *Medium. Got a case of the home-alone blues.*

Wish of the moment: *That I had a boyfriend, a mate, a poltergeist, anyone to keep me company...*

I'm in pain. And I've got no one to blame except dumb old me.

I'd spent such a dull morning rearranging breakfast cereal boxes (at my Saturday job in Tesco, not at home – I'm not *that* sad) that I felt I had to do something drastic just to prove I was still alive. If Shaunna had managed to get the same lunch-break as me (her Saturday job is in Tesco's café), the riskiest thing I might have done was treat myself to an entire family-size bag of mini Snickers for lunch. (Hey, there're nuts in Snickers – plenty of protein!) As it was, I went strolling listlessly around town and found myself being lured into this new, hip hairdressers, with the vague idea that I'd book myself an appointment there to get my hair dyed aubergine or something. And then the funniest thing happened – I somehow found myself back at work, sorting out the dishwasher tablets with a silver bar stud through my slightly swollen eyebrow.

"What made you do that?" Shaunna gasped, when we met up after work.

"They had a special offer on?" I explained lamely, still not entirely sure why the siren call of "Half-price body piercings – this week only!!" had seemed so appealing when I got inside the hairdressers.

"You did *see* that belly button on Josh's sister, didn't you?"

"It's all about hygiene," I said, holding up the bottle of TCP and a bag of salt I'd bought with my supermarket staff discount. "Anyway, why are you lecturing me? *You've* got your belly button pierced!"

Shaunna had the world's most secret piercing for about a year. She knew her mum would have a hyperventilating, hysterical, blubbing fit if she knew Shaunna had got it done, so she lived in tops that were so long they practically skimmed her knees. She finally broke the news to her mum at the beginning of this summer. OK, so she didn't so much *break* the news as get caught lying in the garden with her vest top riding up. Her mum's cool about it now, although for the first couple of months after the belly ring was outed, she did panic that Shaunna was on the verge of joining some anarchist cult and was about to pack in school and spend all her time cultivating dreadlocks.

"I *know* I have a piercing, and I can remember all too well the weeks and weeks I couldn't fasten the top of my trousers 'cause it hurt too much. I just think it's got to be worse when it's on your face, that's all," Shaunna said, eyeing up my egg-sized eyebrow. (*That* scared a few customers off this afternoon, I can tell you.)

"It'll be fine," I assured her, wondering how soon I could take another couple of Nurofen to ease the pain.

And that's been my Saturday so far: rearranging breakfast cereals and restocking the household goods section, with a little self-mutilation to break up the day.

Mmm … so what shall I do now? I could clean the cooker. Or I could do my homework instead of leaving it till tomorrow night. Or I could disinfect my piercing (again). Or I could paint tiny landscapes out of *Lord of the Rings* on my toenails.

God, I'm fed up, if you hadn't noticed. And in pain.

See, this is what sucks about having best mates who are totally loved-up. It gets to Saturday night and all they want to do is hang out on a sofa with their boyfriends, eating kettle chips and cuddling. While here I am, in this draughty old barn of a house, kicking around and wondering how to pass the next few blank hours without boring myself to death.

"Right, I'm out of here!"

I jump at the sound of Helen's voice – I thought she'd left already.

"OK," I shrug from the armchair, giving her outfit a quick checkover. Gap khakis, Timberland boots, an old-faithful fleece-lined denim jacket, a black beanie hat pulled low over her dark, messy bob. "Um, isn't that my hat?"

"Yeah, you don't mind do you? It's started snowing out there and I couldn't find mine."

Somehow, I'm really irritated that she's wearing my hat. Maybe it's 'cause she came in laughing last week, tickled at the fact that that old geezer Mr Watson next door told her he couldn't tell the two of us apart. Well, that might be a super-dooper compliment for Helen, but it's a slap-in-the-face insult to me.

"Whatever," I shrug at her, wishing she'd just go.

"Well, I thought you wouldn't need it if you're not going out tonight."

Rub it in, why don't you. Rub it in that you're off to some amazing party while I'm here with only Cilla Black on the telly and a packet of Bombay Mix for company…

"See you later," Helen calls out, already halfway out the front door, letting an icy blast sneak its way into our house.

"See you…" I mumble, giving a little shiver as the cold settles around my shoulders.

Great.

Now I have peace to sit and fume about the fact that my mother has a better social life than me. It's not as if she goes gallivanting off to dull-as-dishwater dinner parties to talk about house prices, school league tables, the best place to buy sun-dried tomatoes or any other late thirty-something topics that would make my brain melt with boredom. Oh, no. It's the grating fact that my mother has the sort of social life I'd kill for: hanging out with a bunch of student mates, going to student parties, checking out gigs at the student union, hanging out at the union bar … while I'm sitting here in an armchair, aged 17, staring at the ceiling on a Saturday night and wondering if 8 p.m.'s too early to go to bed. (Well, sleeping seems to be a better option than being awake and vegetating.)

It's not that I grudge Helen having a good time (although I do a *tiny* bit, if I'm honest). I mean, she didn't get a chance to do this stuff when she was young, because her mum was on her own and Helen thought she'd be better off working and helping out like her big sister, rather than studying. She met my dad because of that – she was his secretary (yeah, corny, I know) – and then she was married and had me by the time she was twenty. Then when Dad left four years ago, she turned to total mush, never getting out of bed for days on end. I wasn't exactly deliriously happy myself at that time; the first six months after Dad walked out clump together in my memory as this haze of gloom interspersed with visits from my gran and my Aunt Jess, who spent all their time trying to prise Helen out of bed and get us both to eat more than spaghetti hoops on toast (which was all I could face making in my new role as 13-year-old head chef).

Over the next year, my mother started to come back to the real world bit by bit, but the weird thing was, she came back as a completely different person. She got her longish, style-free hair cut short, she chucked the office-friendly smart clothes for jeans and tight-fitting tops, she started sending off for university prospectuses and she asked everyone to stop calling her Mrs Conrad or Mum: it was Helen or nothing.

At first, I quite liked the change; I'd been so scared that she was planning a one-way trip to flip-out land that I was glad to have her back, even if I didn't quite recognize her. And yeah, I was chuffed for her when she got accepted for her course in the History of History or whatever it is she does, and was really pleased when she made loads of new friends at university. I wasn't *quite* so thrilled when I realized all her new friends had an average age of twenty-one and that having a teenage daughter was kind of cramping her style. OK, so she's never exactly *put* it that way, but she treats me more like a flatmate than a daughter now. I mean, what kind of mother says, "How much did that cost? Y'know, I've always fancied a nose ring…" when they first catch sight of your brand new face feature?

But the thing is, I don't even have the same status as a flatmate – normally, you'd invite your flatmate out to any great Saturday night parties you were going to, wouldn't you? Helen never asks me to tag along. Then again, I'd probably say no – partying with your mother is about as bizarre a thought as swapping bikini-wax tips with your teachers.

Excess body hair … *that's* it. Normally I shave my legs, but I've just remembered that Helen got this depilator thing for her last birthday from Aunt Jess (being unperturbed about leg fuzz, she just shoved it in the cupboard under the stairs). This depilator thing; if I remember, it looks like an electric razor, but works like a million rotating tweezers, forcibly yanking the hair out by the roots. Oh, yes; zapping my leg hair could pass a bit of time for me, and the extra pain would suit my present martyr-ish mood really well.

"Where's she put the stupid thing?" I mutter to myself (well, there's no one else to mutter to, is there?), as I nudge aside the hoover in the hall cupboard and start rummaging in an old, tiered vegetable rack that now houses strange things that don't have a home anywhere else in the house. "Tennis shoe whitener... lavender drawer-liners ... money-off tickets to some circus last year ... insoles for wellies... Wait a minute, we don't *have* wellies. What does she keep all this crap for?"

The reason Helen keeps all this crap, of course, is that her life is far too busy and exciting for her nowadays to bother with things like tidying up cupboards. Which is why our place might look quite comfy and nicely done up on the surface, but sneak a peek in any random cupboard or drawer and you're going to find a jumble of red bills, bottle openers, text books and dust-balls. I even found one of Helen's bras in the cutlery drawer last week. When I asked her about it, she said she had her newly washed underwear on the radiator next to our broken tumble-drier, when the repair man turned up to fix it. In a blind panic, she shoved all her smalls in beside the forks and knives, but must have forgotten to retrieve this one bra. Nice try at an excuse. She certainly didn't have one for the time she shoved the walk-about phone in the microwave and put it on a setting for baked potatoes, or the fact that we did without a remote control for the telly for six months till it turned up at the bottom of her sock drawer.

Dad would go mental if he saw all the underground mess and chaos that goes on around here these days. He was always a real place-for-everything-and-everything-in-its-place kind of guy. I thought Helen was like that too, but the minute Dad left, the untidiness started. I think she just had this ditzy gene in her all along, only she suppressed it through the years her and Dad (and me) were together. And Aunt Jess once told me that sharing a room with Helen when they were young was a bit like living in the Bermuda Triangle. You never knew what was going to go missing in this vortex of mess, and you never knew when or where it might pop back up again.

"Gotcha!" I murmur, spotting the (dusty) white and yellow trimmed bag that I know holds the depilator thing. It must have fallen off the towering top tier of jumbled tat and fallen on to this box at the back. A box filled with ... with stuff I haven't seen for a long, *long* time.

I dump the depilator down and stretch over for the box, lifting it towards me and hearing the rattle of plastic CD boxes inside.

He took his toothbrush, he took his clothes, he took every toiletry of his out of the bathroom cabinet. I thought Dad removed every trace of himself when he vanished out of our lives. How come he left his precious music behind...?

Three hours ago, I was contemplating rearranging my nail varnishes in order of popularity to help pass five minutes or so.

Now, time seems to have slipped by at lightning speed, as I've flipped back and forth between tracks on my dad's CD collection (or at least this part that he somehow managed to leave behind), trying to find the songs that remind me most of him. Funny, isn't it? I've spent the last four years training myself to think of him as little as he thinks of us, and yet here I am, feeling my heart ricochet in my chest as the shiny CDs behind faintly familiar band names dredge up memories with every tune. Like this one I've got on now … *Dummy* by Portishead.

"It's spooky. I don't like it," I'd huffed, walking into the living room when Dad was playing their dark, moody dance music.

"Well, *I* do," he'd smiled, scooping up eleven-year-old me in his arms and whirling me around in time to the girl singer crooning over the top of trance beats and slick samples.

I remember I kicked and wriggled so hard to be put back down that he stopped laughing, and thunked me heavily on the floor with a sigh now that I'd sucked all the fun out of the situation.

Poor Dad.

God: "Poor Dad"! What a concept! I've called him a lot of (mostly x-rated) things since he left (and so's Helen), but never anything remotely sympathetic.

But there's always two sides to every story… I hear a traitorous voice whisper somewhere in the back of my head.

It's the same voice that gets me into trouble with creeps like Mitchell McKenzie the other night. The weird thing is, I fall for the voice every time I come within snogging distance of a good-looking loser, even though I should know better. But how come I've always ignored it when it comes to my dad?

I don't know what's wrong with me today – I've been infected by the impetuous bug (or I've just gone *mad* finally). First I go out and get my eyebrow stapled after thinking about it for all of 0.5 seconds, and now I'm scrabbling about in a stupidly messy drawer for the old red address book that I know contains a phone number that I've never tried, and that Helen has only used in emergencies, like when the paternity payment hasn't come through on time.

Omigod. I'm about to call my father. I'd better do it quick before the sane part of me susses out what I'm up to...

chapter three

Every CD tells a story

Date: *Friday 8th November*

Stressometer rating: *Medium–high. Should I admit to my friends how pathetic I am?*

Wish of the moment: *That I'd get over my answerphone addiction...*

"This place is a dump! I love it!" says Adam, grinning as if someone's just told him he's won *Big Brother*.

I can't say I exactly *love* this club; my shoes are sticking to the carpet it's so minging, and I nearly turned and walked out of the loos five minutes ago – only my bladder wasn't as fussy as me. But still, I kind of know what Adam's saying.

"Adam, I don't think anyone's decorated or even *cleaned* this place since 1981," Shaunna says, wrinkling her nose at the padded, red leatherette seat behind us where our coats are piled up, along with Dean's and Molly's. The reason she's scowling at the seat is that all it's fit for is holding coats; the grotty-looking foam stuffing is bulging revoltingly from one dubious-looking, long rip. (Fancy a dance anyone? Or a knife fight, perchance?)

Mind you, even if it is a little on the sleazy (and sticky) side, I have to say that this small, faded venue does have its charms. One of those is the old, ruched velvet curtain that's hanging at the back of the tiny stage in the corner (where the DJ console is presently); add that to the fact that the whole place is decorated in more shades of red (red flock wallpaper, red seats, red swirly carpet) and it has a faint whiff of Moulin Rouge about it. It's also got the faint whiff of stale beer and cats' pee for some strange reason, but we'll skim over that.

The other charm of this place is the people. When Dean invited us along tonight, I hadn't a clue what to expect; all he'd told us – all *he* knew actually – was that Josh (aka Postman Pat) had free tickets to a club-night called "Loaded", run by Josh's older brother Jamie, who's at art school. "Do you think they'll be a bunch of freaks?" Molly had wondered earlier, angsting herself stupid over what to wear. Well, there are a few freaks here, but they're all totally amazing. There's one girl chatting over by the bar with pink and purple dreadlock extensions down to her waist and the most gob-smacking collection of chunky bracelets that go from practically wrist to elbow on both arms. And then there's a black guy who thinks he's Jimi Hendrix, with all this afro hair and a Native-American-style waistcoat thing worn over his long-sleeved black T-shirt. Then there're a couple of goths looking sullen over in the booth at the back, and some punk throwbacks slam-dancing madly to The Strokes right now. (I see they keep bashing into a nervous-looking Molly on the dancefloor.)

Apart from the obvious weirdos – who I love checking out – everyone else looks like your normal, average student type, i.e. exactly who I've always wanted to hang out with. (I mean, exactly who I've wanted to hang out with *apart* from my lovely friends.) The thing is, I know it's only taken me about 30 million lousy dates to figure it out, but I think I've finally had it with lads my own age. They're either a) immature, b) immature but desperate to get their hands down your top (or anywhere else you'll let them) or c) decent, but already taken (think Dean and Adam). I think I need to go out with an older guy next time, some-one who's more laid-back and genuine.

Wonder if there's anyone here tonight who could be interested in little old me? "*Laid-back, genuine student seeks sweet, ditzy girl for fun, laughs and Sunday walks in the park, hand-in-hand…*" Ooh, I like the sound of that. Or maybe I should scribble out my own wanted ad and pin it to the noticeboard over by the phone: "*17-year-old girl, tall, slim, dark hair, seeks thoughtful, fun boy 19+ to help mend dented heart. No creeps, losers, louses or sleazebags.*"

Yeah, that should do it. And I certainly *would* do it, if I happened to have any paper, a pen and the guts to pull it off…

"Wish me luck – I'm going to the loo," Shaunna mutters darkly, slouching away from me and Adam with her arms outstretched and her two index fingers overlapping in the sign of the cross.

"So…" Adam turns the full beam of his attention on me.

Uh-oh – I can feel he's within nanoseconds of making

some joke about my eyebrow piercing, for sure. Fooling around, that's what Adam does best (the day after Josh's party, he didn't so much *take* as *wear* the sumo wrestler suit back to the fancy dress hire-shop on the high street – in broad daylight); but after the week's worth of hassle I've had at school – my new nickname appears to be *Frankenstein*, for God's sake – I don't think I'm in the mood for any more. And anyway, the swelling's gone down and there's only a small scab left so I don't think it looks *too* bad. Well, not under these low lights it doesn't.

"...Shaunna says you tried to phone your dad last Saturday," Adam surprises me by saying instead. "What happened with that?"

There you go: that just proves I'm a truly rotten judge of character. I fall in love with creeps and assume one of my best boy mates wants to tease me stupid for his own amusement, conveniently forgetting that he's actually a really brilliant bloke underneath the goofball exterior.

"Well, I *tried* to phone him," I begin to explain, the fingers of one hand agitatedly twirling themselves into the elasticated bead bracelets on my other wrist. "But I bottled out as soon as his girlfriend answered the phone."

Adam's staring at me, his eyes kind but penetrating. Wonder if he knows there's another part to this story, something I feel too stupid to go blabbing, even to Shaunna and Mol? The fact that I'm such a total saddo that I've phoned back about a million times this week, always withholding my number, always hanging up if *she* answers, all for the weird, twisted high I get from listening to Dad's long-lost voice boom on the answerphone.

I know. Someone help me into a straightjacket *now*...

"That's the woman he left your mum for, right?"

"Right," I shrug. The anonymous woman who Dad never wanted to discuss. I always think it would have been easier for me and Helen if we had a face or name to hate. In the middle of his surprise departure and the vague knowledge of a mystery woman being involved, the only thing me and Helen had been sure of was that we'd both been unceremoniously *chucked*.

"At least, I *suppose* it's still the same one. It's the same contact number he gave Helen after he walked out."

"What would you have said to him if he'd answered the phone?" Adam asks, leaning forward and talking directly into my ear, rather than yell my business out loud against the backdrop of the music.

"God, I hadn't even thought of that!" I realize, at the same time figuring out that I'd better wriggle my fingers free from the tight knots I've twisted in my bracelets, since my middle finger has now gone numb.

What *would* I ask my father? How about...

1) "How come you turned invisible on us overnight?"

2) "Do you feel the slightest, *teeniest* scrap of guilt for walking out on us?"

3) "Would it *kill* you to send a birthday card from time to time? Like on my birthday!"

Or maybe, the way I was feeling on Saturday night, it'd have been...

"Come on, then – let's hear *your* side of the story..."

Adam's saying something soothing, something about how I'll know what to say to my father when the time is right, but I'm suddenly finding it hard to concentrate on his words; a certain song has just started and the tune is burrowing its way into my head. The whole place has gone mad for it, everyone's up dancing, including the freaky girl with the mad extensions and a couple of her cooler-than-cool bloke mates.

"Listen, do you want another drink?" Adam asks.

I think I nod, but my fried brain is distracted, trying to figure out where I know this track from. And then – wham blam – I've got it. It's another of Dad's favourites. It wasn't something from the pile of CDs in the box I rummaged through. This one must have been packed up and taken to his all-new, all-improved life. But back in his *old* life, I remember walking into the living room and watching him and Mum slow-dancing to the sweet classical string part that swoops in between the girl's vocals and the fast dance beats underneath it. That night, they jumped apart like they'd been caught snogging behind the bike shed by the headmaster. At the time, I thought it was a pretty naff sight, but now … well, it's just bizarre to think of them being happy and even flirty towards each other when four years on they're worse than strangers. (By the way, I haven't mentioned coming across that box of CDs to Helen, or my verging-on-the-insane idea of phoning Dad – I don't really want to be the cause of her revisiting the pit of gloom…)

What *is* that track called?

"Same again?"

Adam is wafting an empty glass in front of my face.

"Uh, yeah," I nod vaguely. "Hey, Adam, do you know what this song is…?"

But he's already off, and I can't see Molly and Dean in among the scrum of dancers in front of me. Closest to me

27 ❄ ❄

is that freak girl and her buddies – I could just tap the arm of the guy nearest to me and ask *him*, but he's so trendy-looking he'd probably snarl in my face for not recognizing a classic.

Now the DJ … *he* doesn't look too scary. He looks short, friendly, with short-cropped mousey or gingery hair hidden under a dark Kangol cap worn back to front, but other than the cap, he doesn't look like some hip label snob, or as intimidating as some of the anti-fashion, über-grunge types here either. He's dancing behind the console with a silly grin on his face. I know what he looks like: a hip-hop hamster.

Don't think I'm being mean; ever since I was a kid, I've had this habit of seeing people as animals. I realized from an early age that people take this as a great insult (but, hey, my first primary school teacher *did* look like a walrus) so I've tended to keep my thoughts to myself. I've never told Shaunna that she's a springer spaniel (long, wavy hair, boundless energy, a loyal friend, a taste for Pedigree Chum – OK, I made that last part up), or mentioned to Molly that she's a dead ringer for the white angora guinea pig I used to look after at weekends in Primary Four. And me? Tall, skinny, peanut for a brain… I'm an emu, of course.

"Um…" I mumble, sidling up to the edge of the stage.

The oblivious DJ keeps right on dancing, while slipping a record back into its sleeve.

"Excuse me!" I try a little louder.

That worked. He turns and smiles down at me, raising his eyes questioningly.

"What is this track?" I ask, but see immediately from his frown that he can't hear.

He motions me to come up on the stage, and with a tug at my long, tight denim skirt, I stride up the couple of steep steps to the stage beside him and feel almost giddy looking out at the different perspective the room suddenly takes on. Instead of grotty, the heaving mass of dancers makes it look almost groovy; almost like a real club, instead of the Moulin Rouge meets the local council tip.

"You all right?"

"Yeah, yeah, sorry!" I feel myself flushing. "It just looks so much better from up here!"

I'm taller than him by about five centimetres, I notice, even in my trainers.

"Huh! I don't know about that!" DJ Hamster smiles at me. "I can't help imagining it with all the usual punters who used this place until recently!"

It's my turn to frown at him.

"Loads of seedy guys," he attempts to explain to me. "This place used to be a strip joint. The girls danced up here. That pole you're leaning on was part of their act!"

I hadn't even realized I'd been holding on to the slender, brass pole that came between me and DJ Hamster, but instantly, I whip it away and wish I carried a handbag sized bottle of bleach around with me.

"Anyway, can I help you with something?" he laughs at my obvious horror. "You want a request?"

"No ... sorry if I sound thick, but what's this track you're playing?"

"'Unfinished Sympathy' by Massive Attack," he replies, as the familiar name slots into some puzzle in the muddle of my mind. "It's from their first album. Why – do you like it?"

DJ Hamster is fearlessly leaning on the pole now, as if he's got all the time in the world (and no fear of strange germs).

"It was just one of my dad's favourites," I find myself telling him, when really I could have just said "Yes" and sloped off back to my friends. Instead I relax a little, and even feel a flutter of excitement when I spot a few girls on the dancefloor turning to check out who the DJ's chatting to. Suddenly I don't feel so much of an awkward emu and the DJ boy doesn't look quite so much like a cuddly rodent.

"Well, your dad's got very good taste," he nods appreciatively. "What else is he into?"

"Um… Tricky, Portishead, that kind of moody dance stuff. And a lot of old rock too, like The Smashing Pumpkins and—"

"Hold on, um…?"

He seems to be turning back to his decks but he's looking expectantly at me too. It takes a few seconds for my peanut brain to figure out that he's waiting for me to tell him my name.

"Jude," I blurt out quickly.

"Nice…" he nods. "But listen, I've just got to line the next track up."

"Oh … I better go," I begin flustering.

"You don't have to!"

I like that smile – it's friendly and warm. But all of a sudden I feel like I'm in a goldfish bowl up here (it's not my imagination; a bunch of girls really *are* staring, *hard*).

"I'll catch you later, um…?"

Yep, I nicked his trick.

"Gareth. Or Gaz. I don't mind which," he grins, fixing his headphones to his ears. "But anytime you fancy a visit, me and the lap-dance pole are always here! Well, tonight and every Friday from now on!"

Amazingly for me, my legs manage not to get tangled on the way down, and I find myself shifting through the crowded dancefloor till I'm back with Shaunna and Adam, just in time to take my drink from him.

"*He* looks nice," Shaunna tilts her head towards the DJ. Gareth. Gaz.

"He is nice. At least I *think* he's nice."

"So how come you've got that glow?"

"What glow?" I ask her, slapping my hands on my face for signs of any telltale "glowing".

"The 'ooh-I-could-quite-fancy-him' glow!" giggles Shaunna. "I mean, he's not your type! You said yourself you don't go for nice guys!"

I glance over towards Gareth and catch his eye straight away – he gives me a grin and a quick thumbs-up.

Shaunna's right. He's OK-looking, not drop-dead gorgeous; he's friendly, not charming or arrogant; he's shorter than me, and I've never given shorter guys a second thought. He's everything I've never fancied in a boy before.

And yet…

"I told you, I need a new type," I turn and tell Shaunna in as definite a voice as I can manage.

"Yeah, yeah, and I'm the new Kate Moss," Shaunna rolls her eyes. "Anyway, Adam was saying you two were talking about your dad before. So what are you thinking – are you going to try and call him again?"

What, *more* than the five million times I've called him this week already?

"I don't know," I shake my head. "It's been years – I don't know what his situation is now, or even what he looks like any more…"

From the answerphone message, I know that his voice is the same, but he could have grown a beard, gone grey, gone bald, had a facelift, had a spiderweb tattooed on his forehead for all I know. And every day that he isn't around, I find it harder and harder to fix a picture of him in my mind. And that's the only place I *will* find a picture of him because I chucked out every photo I had of him in a mad strop about a month after he left. Turned out Helen had done exactly the same…

"Why don't you go and see him?"

"B-Because," I stammer, shocked at Shaunna's suggestion, "we've only got a phone number – I don't know where he lives."

"Yeah?" Adam butts in. "I think I *just* might be able to help you out there…"

Omigod. What's he got in mind? The last thing I need is Adam Pindar turning detective and going undercover for my benefit. Everything could get a lot more complicated if my dad suddenly finds himself being stalked by a sumo wrestler…

chapter four

All roads lead to...?

Date:	*Sunday 10th November*
Stressometer rating:	*High. Will I faint before I freeze to death?*
Wish of the moment:	*A touching reconciliation and a hot bath, please.*

Adam's plan for tracking down my father was both stunning and cunning.

We'd gone back to Shaunna's for a coffee after the club on Friday, when he launched Phase One of the plan: Research.

"There you go!" he'd said, presenting me with Phase Two: The Evidence. "Is that the phone number you tried? 'Cause if it is, then this is the right Peter Conrad and this is his address."

Oh, yes, it had taken Adam all of three minutes to grab the Sullivan's copy of the phone directory and look up Peter Conrad in the listings.

Good grief … why hadn't *I* thought of something that obvious? Why hadn't I realized that my super-efficient, super-organized father would *of course* be registered in the local residential phone book?

Because I have a peanut for a brain. Told you.

"They don't like strangers round these parts," Shaunna mutters darkly, like she's auditioning for the role of a suspicious yokel in an Agatha Christie murder mystery.

She's referring to the two old ladies whose brisk Sunday morning stroll has been disrupted by the fact that they've encountered two teenage delinquents (i.e. us) slouching suspiciously on the bench beside the rose bushes. And it's not just the old ladies who've been checking us out – there were three little boys who stopped dead and stared at us for minutes on end as if we'd just crash-landed from the Planet Tharg. We've even had a lightly growling collie come over and sniff us for illicit drugs/stolen gems/arms caches before it finally trotted off through the park gate with one final threatening growl in our direction.

Eastbury Road: that's where that park gate opens on to, and "24 Eastbury Road" happens to be what's scribbled on the little piece of paper in my coat pocket. I think my fingers are wrapped around it, but I'm not sure – my gloves are too thick to make out anything that flimsy.

(God, if Helen only knew where I was…)

24 Eastbury Road. I can't really get it to sink into this dozy head of mine that *this* is where my dad actually lives – and that I'm here, right now, outside his house. (OK, so there's a road, a park railing and a bunch of bushes – rosy and otherwise – between me and the modern, Barratt's-style

house, but who's going to get picky over details like that?)

"So…" Shaunna turns her attention away from the alarmed pensioners (now clutching their handbags tightly) and goes back to what we were saying before we were so rudely ogled at. "Do you really like this guy, then?"

I think Shaunna's plan is to twitter away inanely for as long as she can this morning to distract me from fainting through sheer panic. Maybe it's a sensible enough plan but it's getting on my wick. We've already discussed what was on telly last night, how naff the pale pink leather suite is that her sister Ruth's just bought for her flat, and whether or not the ominous black clouds hovering above us are going to chuck it down any minute.

"I only spoke to him for a couple of minutes on Friday night, so I don't know if I *really* like him," I tell my friend through slightly gritted teeth. "I just thought he seemed interesting, that's all!"

We're talking about Gareth the DJ now. I bet she thinks this'll definitely take my mind off the fact that we are currently freezing our limbs off sitting on a park bench in a small market town an hour's train journey from civilization (i.e. home).

"*I* know – why don't we get Dean to find out more about him? He could ask Josh to ask his brother Jamie, and Jamie's bound to know Gareth pretty well since he hired him to play at the club. Maybe—"

"Shaunna, I can't think about that stuff right now. OK?"

What I mean is, my head is too stuffed with tangled-up thoughts of how I'll feel if I *do* catch a glimpse of my dad. And will a glimpse be enough? Or will I find myself sprinting over to him, screaming at him that I hate him or throwing myself into his arms and telling him I miss him? Or both?

I suddenly realize that Shaunna is looking slightly deflated, and now I feel like a rat. I didn't mean to bite her head off, it's just that my nerves are so shredded it's like they've been shoved through a mincer. And back.

"Jude … you've just *had* one," she murmurs, nodding at the cigarette that I've just thrown on the tarred path and stamped out.

"Well, I'm having this one now," I say shakily, lighting up another cigarette from my fast-dwindling packet of ten.

God, I *hate* the fact that I smoke. But honestly, I only do it when I'm stressed. (Shaunna once said that I must be stressed 50% of the time, then, if that's my excuse. Well, maybe I am.)

Shaunna turns away and stares through the foliage at the blue front door we've been watching. I think she's gone silent because 1) it's dawned on her that I'm slightly tetchy today (*and* the rest), and 2) she knows there's no point giving me the please-stop-smoking lecture because we've been here about a million times before.

At least Molly's not here. (She couldn't come with us on our spying mission, what with it being her kid sister's birthday and everything.) If she was here and saw how many cigarettes I was getting through she'd be doling out endless facts to make me go *eek!* – along the lines of: "Did you know you're 24 times more likely to get lung cancer?/Did you know there's ammonia and carbon monoxide in cigarette smoke?/Did you know that me and Shaunna have a 10–30% higher risk of getting cancer 'cause of the passive smoking we do around you?"

Today, of all days, I don't need the guilt-trip. My heart's fixing to explode with this anxiety attack I'm trying to suppress, so if I keel over dead then I won't have to worry about the dangers of smoking anyway…

"Hey, didn't we pass a petrol station on the main street, just when we came out of the station?" asks Shaunna, all hunched up in her coat and stamping her feet to stave off frostbite. God, I wish *I'd* worn my cosy Afghan coat instead of just this bum-freezing padded jacket.

"Why – do you fancy a gallon of super-unleaded or something?" I try and joke, faintly amazed that I've managed a passing attempt at humour in the state I'm in.

"No. I just thought they might have a coffee machine. I could nip up there just now and get us—"

"Don't go!" I squealed, instant panic chilling my already frozen bones. "You can't leave me on my own!"

I'm a self-confessed wimp at the best of times, but I couldn't carry off a *second* of this by myself. If one more person (or dog) stares at me weirdly, I'm liable to start sobbing. And if that door opened while Shaunna was gone … well, I need a witness to what my dad looks like in case I pass out before I get a good nosey.

"Fine! OK! I won't go anywhere!" Shaunna tries to reassure me.

Ooh, that feels good. Not the reassurance bit; that hasn't worked at all – but the fact that she's put a comforting arm around my shoulder. Snuggling together may be the only way to make sure neither of us dies from exposure. Then again, we'd better not; it'll just make the locals look at us even *more* strangely. They'll probably phone the police and get us arrested for Loitering With Intent To Snuggle. Could you imagine it? The first glimpse my father has of me after all these years is a mugshot in the local paper under "Crime Round-up".

"Hey, look!" Shaunna whispers sharply, pointing a finger on the hand that isn't attached to the arm currently around my shoulders. "The door…!"

The blue door is opening. I couldn't be more enthralled if it had just disintegrated into a million twinkling stars and fluttered out into the atmosphere.

I'm about to maybe, hopefully, possibly, *unbelievably* … see my dad!

"Jude! What are you doing!" I hear Shaunna hissing as I leap off the bench, run at gazelle-like speeds over the grass and hurtle myself commando-style into the rhododendron bushes that ring the park.

I crouch down on my haunches, my eyes fixed on the door, which is still only slightly open. Through the glass panels on either side of it, I can make out a figure or figures moving, getting ready to leave.

"I just wanted a closer look!" I whisper my reply to Shaunna's question, as I hear her crashing noisily into the bushes behind me.

"Can you see anything yet?"

Shaunna is bobbing and weaving, trying to get a clear view.

"Yes! It's opening wider! Here he— oh."

Most *definitely* "oh".

I know I'd doodled with the idea that my dad might have a beard or be bald by now, but I hadn't actually planned on him being Asian…

* * *

"I don't get it. It was the right house, so what was that family doing there?"

I don't answer Shaunna's question, not just because I don't have an answer to it but because my teeth are chattering so hard that speech is beyond me.

We'd hovered in the bushes for ages, watching the Asian family lock up and pile in their top-of-the-range people carrier. Then we'd hovered some more when I realized that the entire back seam of my jeans had ripped open when I'd launched into my commando assault into the bushes. I knew that having your knickers on show in the park would probably get us arrested for Indecent Exposure ("Local Man's Secret Daughter Caught Flashing!"), so I'd ended up hauling my jersey off and wrapping it round my waist to hide my modesty. Which means, of course, that I'm now braving the Arctic temperatures (and the sudden downpour that's just come on) in a T-shirt and a padded jacket that might as well be padded with *air* for all the heat it's keeping in.

"Let me see that bit of paper again," says Shaunna, holding out her gloved hand as we hurry along the road that'll lead us to the station. *And* the warm train, *and* the buffet car, *and* all the hot drinks that £7.50 can buy … bliss.

"It's the right address!" I insist through chattering teeth, as I rifle in my pocket for the slip of paper with my bare hand. (Managed to lose my gloves in the bushes when I was taking my jersey off. Smart move, I *don't* think.) "There you go!"

"Jude, you idiot! This says '24 Eastbury *Street*', not Eastbury *Road*! We were staking out the wrong house! Look – look at that sign there on the corner. *That's* Eastbury Street!"

I can hear what Shaunna's saying but my eyes are currently fixed on a dark-haired man – in his 40s – unloading bulging supermarket plastic bags out of the back of a car and handing them to a blonde woman who grabs them and hurries through the rain to the shelter of an open front door.

"Shaunna…"

That's all I can manage to mutter as my gaze becomes superglued to the sight of the man halfway-down Eastbury Street who is now slamming the boot of his car shut and walking around to the back passenger door.

"Is it…?"

"Yes," I whisper.

I'm too far away to see his features clearly, but there's something about his shape and the way he moves; of course it's him. Of course it's my father.

And that … that bundle he's taking out of the back seat; it looks like a baby…

"Oh, Jude!" says a voice that belongs to Shaunna, but it sounds weird, like it's warped or fuzzy or something. Or maybe it's just my brain that's gone warped and fuzzy.

I want to turn to my best friend and discuss what this might mean: is it a neighbour's kid? A friend's? A special free offer they got for spending more than £100 at Sainsbury's?

But I take one look at Shaunna's stunned features and know that I have to apply her boyfriend's logic here: the Adam Pindar Theory, which states that The Simplest Explanation Is Probably True.

Yep, I think I've just had my first glance at my half-brother. Or half-sister.

Wow, that pavement's coming up at me very fast…

chapter five

Slightly dented, body and soul

Date:	*Friday 15th November*
Stressometer rating:	*High. Can't get my dad (or that bundle of baby) out of my mind...*
Wish of the moment:	*Not to end up with any more scars on my face.*

Ten seconds ago, I gasped when I caught sight of my reflection in the chipped mirror above the scuzzy sink in the grotty, unflatteringly lit club loos.

Mmm, I looked *gorgeous*, what with the scab on my left (pierced) eyebrow and the sticking plaster barely covering the splatter of grazed skin above my right one. Thank God I hadn't needed stitches; that'd *really* get the Frankenstein nickname sticking at school. But that tiny cut had bled madly – when I woke up from my five-second fainting fit, Shaunna's face had been white as a sheet with panic. It was only after she'd washed the worst of the blood away in the station toilet that we both realized the damage wasn't too bad. At least the *physical* damage I'd just endured.

And on the emotional side, well, in case you were wondering, I didn't go and confront my dad last Sunday, not under the circumstances.

And those circumstances were...

1) I didn't have the nerve to.

2) Him and the baby had disappeared inside the house by the time I'd come round.

3) Turning up on your long-lost father's doorstep dripping blood from a head wound is perhaps a little over-dramatic for a first meeting. (Lucky my forehead broke my fall when I fainted, huh?)

And so I've felt in serious mope mode all this week, not sure if seeing him – even just from a distance – was a good idea or a very, very *bad* one. Considering the fact that there's now the complication of a mystery baby and I'd say it was *definitely* a very, very bad one...

"Are you coming or going?" I'm vaguely aware of someone asking me.

Good question. My world seems so upside-down right now that I feel a little like Alice in Wonderland, tumbling in slow motion down a long burrow filled with vaguely familiar things: school; my friends; Helen's strange household filing system (I found a Dove deodorant and a gas bill in the fridge last night). But I'm viewing all of them as if I'm peering through the wrong end of a pair of binoculars. I can't remember the last time I felt so weird. Oh, yes I can – it was when Dad first left home...

"I *said*, are you coming or going?"

A tallish guy with a super-trendy, super-indie hairdo and a snarling expression is staring impatiently at me.

"Neil, a simple 'Excuse me' usually works. Be nice!" a girl right behind him says.

All of a sudden, I realize that I've ground to a standstill in the doorway that leads from the club room through to the loos. I'm blocking everyone's way, and looking like a moron into the bargain. Quickly, I stand to one side to let these two people past.

"I was just trying to be *funny*, Anya!" the lad who spoke first says to the girl with amazing hair.

"Didn't sound like that to me, Neil!" the girl called Anya tells him as they walk by me. "Don't mind him – he can be *such* a grouch!"

She directs that last part to me, with a grin and a toss of her long pink and purple raggedy extensions and a rattle of her million bracelets.

"Hey! I am *not* a grouch!" the guy called Neil protests to his friend, sounding suddenly a lot less cool than he looks.

Then they're both gone before I can respond with more than a wan smile, and I feel even *that* half-hearted effort quickly slip off my face as I scan the heaving crowd on the dancefloor for any sign of my friends. I shouldn't have come here tonight – I'm not in the mood, and I must be about as much fun to hang out with as a Manchester United fan who's watching them lose to the local school's under-10s team.

Maybe I should just get my coat and sneak away home, without giving Shaunna and Mol the chance to persuade me to stay. No – bad idea; they might think I've been abducted or beamed up by aliens or something equally worrying.

Or … I *could* go and speak to Gareth the DJ, since he

appears to be smiling and waving me to come over. (Ooh, is that a genuine grin I suddenly sense slipping on to my face?)

I'm such an idiot.

In the space of three songs, I've managed to tell a virtual stranger every personal detail of my life. Well, OK, not stuff like what my bra size is or the fact that I've had a life-long crush on John Travolta, even though he's a spooky scientologist and has a tendency to be on the pudgy side these days. But I *have* managed to bore Gareth stupid about the situation with my dad: about him leaving, about me stalking him, about me keeping it all (including the existence of a small baby) from Helen…

"Here," he says, passing me a crushed paper tissue he's rooted around for in the pocket of the jacket that's tossed on the stool behind him.

I'm not making *too* much of a show of myself – I'm not sobbing exactly – but he's spotted the trickle of a tear that's trying to squeeze its way out of my eye.

Isn't he sweet?

God, I hope Gareth's not regretting motioning me over earlier, thinking he's got some troubled, hysterical girlie on his hands…

("What's up? You're not looking too happy tonight. And, hey – what happened to your head?" That's how he'd started the conversation off and that's when I'd started pouring my heart out to him.)

The thing is, I can hardly believe it but he doesn't seem embarrassed or bored by what I'm saying. In fact, he's being really sympathetic and kind. Excuse me if I'm shocked, but I've never known a boy to be like that; well, more precisely, I've never known a boy *who I've fancied* to be like that.

Oh, yes, I've fallen. How can I resist?

"I don't know what your dad's problem is – even if he and your mum weren't getting along, he should still have stayed in touch with you!"

See? For quarter of an hour, this is the kind of perfect, understanding thing Gareth's been coming out with.

"I mean, you *are* his daughter. He's mad to be missing out on knowing you!" he says, lightly touching my back with his broad, comforting hand as he bends forward to talk to me. "Oh, hold on – I have to cue up the next track…"

Gareth's arms, I notice – as he expertly flips a record out of its sleeve and on to the decks – seem strong, thick and muscly, and they're covered in the same fine, sandy-brown hair that he wears close cropped under his Kangol cap. He is *so* not my type, but suddenly I can't remember liking anyone more than this kind boy with the gentle face and soft, hazel eyes shining out at me from a halo of pale, long lashes.

"The only thing Dean managed to find out about Gareth," I remember Molly telling me earlier tonight, as I stare out now across the bobbing heads on the dancefloor, "is that he's in his first year at art school. Oh, and that he was going out with someone for ages, but they split up not very long ago…"

That's not a lot to go on, but it's OK, I think to myself, only vaguely aware of the curious looks some girls are giving me from down on the dancefloor (probably curious to see who the Frankenstein chick is who's chatting up the DJ).

In fact, those small shreds of info were *more* than OK. Gareth goes to art school, which means he's creative. He went out with someone for ages, which must mean he's dependable and loyal. And he's not going out with whoever it was any more, which is the best shred of information of all.

And in a strange way, I even quite like the slightly jealous looks I'm getting from the girls on the dancefloor – no one's ever been jealous of any boys I've hung out with before, mainly because most girls tend to be smarter than me and know not to go near them with a bargepole.

But that was then and this is now.

"Feeling better?" Gareth asks me, slipping his headphones off now that the next track has kicked in, and reaching for one of my hands with both of his.

"Oh, *yes*," I smile shyly, a shot of electricity shooting up my arm from his fingers and sending my whole nervous system tingling.

Don't they say every cloud has a silver lining? Maybe – just maybe – Gareth could be the silver lining to my megastressed week...

chapter six

Taking the blame...

Date: *Saturday 16th November*

Stressometer rating: *Medium. Finding your house invaded is pretty irritating.*

Wish of the moment: *That I had a nice, mumsy mum, instead of a Helen...*

Gwyneth Paltrow. Wouldn't you just like to shake her? It's like that craggy old actor Sean Connery; he can only act in a Scottish voice, whether he's playing a Spanish conquistador, an American archaeologist or a Russian U-boat captain. With Gwyneth, she can only play *wet*. And we've just wasted a quality girls-only video night watching her be wet, soppy and sad-eyed yet again...

"Sorry that film was so crap," Molly shrugs, stuffing the rented video into the roomy pocket of her coat.

We're standing chatting on the pavement outside Shaunna's, with a soft swirling of snow drifting prettily in the beam of the street lamp and settling on to our shoulders like frozen dandruff.

"It's not your fault," I shiver, wearing only a thin fleece since my house is just across the road.

Actually, it *is* Molly's fault, but it seems petty to bring that up. What with me and Shaunna busy working at the supermarket all day (hard-going since we stayed at the club so late last night), we'd entrusted Molly to grab something decent from the video shop before the teatime rush cleared the shelves of all the new releases. And what did she bring back? Something drippy with Gwyneth-soggy-Paltrow in it, who Shaunna in particular can't stand. ("Oh, for God's sake, stop whingeing, you big, gangly wimp!") It's a pity it wasn't a better movie, really, as getting my girl-friends to myself on a Saturday night is a pretty rare occurrence these days, since it's gradually turned into cosy couple territory. The reason I'd been granted this special dispensation was because Dean and Adam had been glued to some crucial football match on TV tonight, leaving Shaunna and Molly at a loose end.

But we'd still managed to have a good time, lounging and lazing in Shaunna's room chatting about the club last night (and *no*, nothing exactly *happened* with Gareth, apart from lots of chatting up close and then grinning at each other from a distance), and stuff about the situation with my dad and how I feel about it. (The answer to that is: I don't know, and keep changing my mind about it every five seconds... Oh, yes, I'm as wet and wimpy as Gwyneth Paltrow.)

"Hey, looks like it's all going off at your place tonight!" Molly suddenly breaks off and nods her head at something over my snow-covered shoulder. "You never said Helen was having a party!"

"Probably because I didn't know she was," I grumble, turning and checking out the figures moving in the lit-up bay window of our front room.

I'd been aware of the drifting sound of music when we'd left Shaunna's two minutes ago, but I'd presumed it was coming from some bass-laden stereo in a mini-cab or car parked up and waiting outside someone's house.

"Have a good time!" Molly jokes, walking backwards away from me and waving her gloved hand.

"I won't!" I joke back, starting to cross the road for home. "At least, not till I lock myself in my room!"

And then Molly's gone, disappearing into a swirl of thickening snow in the darker spots between the spaced-out street lamps.

Ooh, I'm so not in the mood for one of Helen's dos. Specially since she didn't even warn me about this one, I think to myself, yanking the zip at my neck higher as I hurry through the freezing night air towards my front gate. *If she'd told me, I could have slept over at Shaunna's and avoided it all.*

Too late for that now. Maybe it was only a few minutes since I'd left Shaunna's house, but it would definitely be out of order to go trudging back there with my PJs and my toothbrush – her mum and dad were on their way to bed when me and Molly were leaving, and we'd heard them tell Shaunna to double lock the door and put the lights out when she'd seen us off. Mr and Mrs Sullivan; they're the kind of old-fashioned parents who wouldn't appreciate their routine being shaken by unexpected late-night door-bell ringing or me and Shaunna lugging the spare mattress and bedding along the corridor in the middle of the night.

At least what passes for the middle of the night to them…

It's obviously still early, as far as the people yelling and laughing in my living room are concerned.

"Hey, Jude!" Helen calls out when she spots me standing in the doorway surveying the scene.

She doesn't mean it that way, but hearing her call out my name like that gets some joker breaking into song, and then a few other jokers join in. I get that all the time, but that's usually down to brain-dead guys at school, not a bunch of students who should know better. I mean, I know I *love* The Beatles' "Hey, Jude", especially since I was named after it and everything, but it really wears you down when people turn it into a big hoot at my expense.

"No wait – Jude!" Helen calls out, seeing that I'm about to barge off up the stairs.

I hover for a second, in case she's got something genuinely important to say, and catch a glimpse of something that makes me feel slightly queasy. The guy sitting beside her? He's OK-looking, dressed in faded black everything, but he must be in his early twenties. There's nothing wrong with that as such, but when Helen broke away from him there, I realized that they hadn't just been chatting – they'd been holding hands…

"Listen, you haven't seen the bottle-opener anywhere, have you, Jude?" she asks me, with the same level of concern on her face as if she was saying, "Where were you, Jude? I was worried about you!" Good to know where her priorities lie.

"No idea," I shrug and take a few steps towards the staircase.

In fact, I *do* have an idea where the stupid bottle-opener

is – I watched Helen use it to wedge the back door open this morning when she was taking some rubbish out to the bin. It's probably still kicking around gathering dust on the kitchen floor right now.

"Pity," says Helen, wrinkling up her nose in disappointment. "It's taking Alastair ages to open the wine with his Swiss Army knife… Still, we've managed with that so far. Do you want a glass?"

"No, thanks," I reply, noticing that she's pinned her dark bob back behind one ear with a couple of flower-shaped, diamanté clips. Doesn't she understand that it's against the law for anyone over the age of eighteen to shop in Claire's Accessories?

"Or a beer?"

"No. You didn't tell me you were having a party tonight."

"Well, it's not really a *party*, Jude, I didn't *plan* it. It's just a case of everyone piling back here once the pub shut."

Not for the first time, I wish that I had a boring, ordinary mother like Shaunna's, whose idea of a great Saturday night is watching telly, maybe going wild and having a few chocolates, then straight to bed with a nice crime thriller to read. Instead, I have a mother who likes impromptu "gatherings". And no matter what she calls it, there'll still be plenty of party debris to clear up tomorrow morning…

"Sure you don't want a beer or something, Jude?"

I start trudging up the stairs, shaking my head, partly in answer to her question and partly at the idea of me actually hanging out with all her friends. "Hi – yes, I'm 17. Do you realize how old that makes Helen? Yes, it's funny when you think that *we're* closer in age than you and

Helen..." That would be a weird conversation to have, wouldn't it? Specially with the young guy who was holding her hand in there.

I guess Helen gets the message, and turns back to her party, while I head for my room.

My hand automatically searches the wall for the light switch, but something makes me stop. I slip into the darkness, close the door behind me and feel myself drawn over to the view out of the window – it's beautiful. The night sky has that orange glow you get when fluffy blankets of snow clouds hang low over cities, reflecting the light back down on to the streets and houses. Those clouds are spilling their contents hard now, and the snow is swirling over Westburn Park, its trees and bushes dark and dense, but lit by pools of soft yellow from the Victorian street lamps that are dotted along the meandering footpaths. Surrounding the park, there's a jumbled trail of what looks like fairy lights strung out above the silhouetted treetops, blinking and twinkling through the torrents of white flakes. By day, all that's there are some dull blocks of flats and concrete high-rises to spoil the view; tonight, the brightness shining from their hundreds of windows makes everything seem magical, like a wonderland. I take a deep breath, as if that'll somehow help me hold the memory of this amazing scene in my head and then—

Then I'm aware of a shrill, incessant ringing above the blare of Joni Mitchell singing at full volume. (Helen's choice – it has to be. No one else down in my living room is old enough to know who Joni Mitchell is unless, like me, they've got a *parent* who's into her.)

"Someone *please* answer the door…" I mutter softly, not in any hurry to leave the sanctity of my room and go stomping downstairs only to open the front door to another of Helen's party guests.

But the stop-start ringing continues, as does Joni's song, and the noise of laughter and chattering voices overlapping each other.

"I'm not answering it!" I say defiantly to myself.

Of course, within about ten seconds, my resolve has evaporated, and I'm hauling the door open to one very irate old man in a dressing gown that looks like it's been made out of one of those corny tartan travelling rugs you used to get.

"Hello, Mr Watson," I say warily, while trying to smile a neighbourly smile.

I don't like this man at the best of times (him *or* his snooty, grumpy wife), and – maybe it's the time of night, or the dressing gown, or the fact that he's frowning so hard his hairy grey eyebrows are meeting in the middle – I somehow doubt whether he's come for a pleasant chat about the proposed new residents' recycling bins. (Which he and his wife are against, of *course*, because they're always against *everything*.)

"Young lady!" he blusters, and in that one bluster my heart sinks. "Some of us are trying to sleep! Can you please turn that music down!"

"But it isn't my—"

"You know, I just don't understand what your mother's playing at, letting a girl of your age have house parties, inviting who knows what kind of people into the neighbourhood!"

"But, Mr Watson – it's nothing to do with—"

"I've no more to say. I'll be having a word with your mother in the morning about this!"

And with that, the moany old git tramples back down our path, retracing the prints his slippers have left in the soft covering of settled snow.

Great – not only has my house been taken over by noisy strangers, but I'm now being blamed for depriving the local OAPs of their sleep…

I slam the door hard, hoping to make some impact on the party animals inside, but it works about as well as blowing a referee's whistle just as a twenty-one gun cannon salute is going off.

"Helen!" I try yelling from the doorway.

It's no use – the music's been turned up louder than it was when I first came over from Shaunna's. Anyway, Helen seems preoccupied by her toy-boy, who is now – omigod! – leaning over to kiss her!

Right, that's it. I storm into the living room, weaving past clusters of chattering people, and wallop the volume control on the stereo from ten down to one.

"Awwwww!"

"What's going on?"

"What's happened to the music?"

I ignore the chorus of drunken-sounding protests and stare hard at my slightly–startled looking mother. (I'm blanking the guy by her side.)

"I've just had Mr Watson at the door complaining," I bark at her. "So keep it down!"

Still shaking with the rage I feel at being wrongly accused, I turn and head for the door, not interested in having any kind of conversation with her right now – not when she's so "busy"…

Everyone stands aside silently, parting to let me leave. Only it's not quite silent – those are definitely snickers I can hear.

"OK, *Mum*! We'll be really quiet, promise, *Mum*!" comes a voice dripping with sarcasm somewhere behind me, and the snickers turn into full-on laughs.

I can't get out of this room and up the stairs fast enough…

How dare they? How dare they make a fool of me like that? I hate the fact that I've had to come over all super-boring and responsible just because my mother can't be *bothered* to.

Halfway up the stairs, I look back down at the phone on the hall table. Crouching down, I slip my hand through the banister and make a grab for it, before I hurry up the last few stairs to my room.

It's late; he's bound to be home – he's got a kid, hasn't he?

After all, maybe my other parent is more conscientious than the one I've got at home. Maybe there's even a good reason why he's kept my new baby brother or sister secret.

And right here, right now, I'm going to give my dad the chance to explain everything to me…

chapter seven

Long time no see

Date:	*Saturday 23rd November*
Stressometer rating:	*High. Higher than high. I'm so excited I can hardly breathe...*
Wish of the moment:	*That I'll manage to find the words to talk to him.*

I can't believe Shaunna hasn't turned up for work today. Yeah, I know she's been ill – she didn't make it to the club last night with us – but I really, *really* needed to talk to her today. How can I get through this lunchtime without her?

"Shaunna?"

"Jude? Where are you?" says a croaky, nasal-sounding voice.

"I'm in the bus shelter outside Tesco's," I tell her.

I couldn't phone her from the staff canteen – there's a no smoking policy and right now I *definitely* need to have a cigarette...

"But it's … it's hideous out there, isn't it? I can see hailstones outside my window…"

"Yeah," I agree, narrowing my eyes against the biting wind and watching hailstones practically the size of Brussels sprouts bounce off the road in front of me. "That's why I'm sitting in the bus shelter."

"So … what's up?" Shaunna sniffles. "How was the club last night? I haven't heard from Adam yet. Did you have a good time? Is there any more gossip on you and Gareth?"

"Nothing too exciting. I mean, it was great – he came over and talked to me on his break."

Exciting would be if Gareth asked me out (I wish), but I guess right now, I'm still getting a big kick from all the chatting and flirting stuff we're doing every week.

"What did you talk about?"

"About people in the club and stuff, mostly. Oh, and then he introduced me to that girl with the pink and purple dreadlocks. Her name's Anya – she's really nice."

She *was* nice. I know it's dumb to get won over by a compliment, but the first thing Anya said to me was that she loved my boots, and maybe it is a bit pathetic, but I warmed to her straight away after that. Didn't warm to her friends much though; the two so-cool-it-hurts boys I've seen her hang around with before and some sour-faced girl trying to hang a pose straight out of *The Face* magazine. They all managed uninterested "hi"s in my direction, after Gareth introduced them as Ben, Neil (the sarky, deeply unfunny guy whose path I'd blocked on the way to the loos last week) and *Saffron*, for God's sake.

"She does look pretty interesting," Shaunna agrees, and I'm so lost in thought that it takes me a second to work out what she's agreeing with me about – and then I remember it's Anya.

"Yeah, well, I'm not phoning to tell you about the club…" I tell her, feeling my heart rate soar with the secret I'm about to spill.

"Oh, yeah? What's up?"

"Guess who called me this morning! On my mobile! On the way to work!"

"Homer Simpson?"

"*Shaunna!*" I squeak irately.

How can she fool around about something so mind-blowing? Oh – hold on; I haven't told her what it is yet…

"Aw, Jude … sorry, but this flu's made my head turn to mush. Go on, just tell me!"

"My dad!"

"Omigod!"

There – that got her. I mean, she knew already that I spoke to him on the phone last Saturday night. She knew every second of that ten-second phone call; the way my dad went silent and then sheepish on me, then told me hurriedly that he couldn't talk, but to give him my mobile number quick, and that he'd call me during the week, when he got a chance. She knew that I'd been going out of my mind with worry ever since then, torturing myself with reasons why every call that came through wasn't from him. And now, finally, he'd phoned me…

"I know!" I can't help but giggle, thudding my feet up and down on the pavement like an over-excited school-kid and getting a strange look from the bus driver who pulls up beside me and wonders why I'm not getting on (too busy acting like a nutter and giggling in the midst of a hailstorm). "Can you believe it?!"

"*And?*" Shaunna asks. "What did he say?"

Not much. It had been another lightning-quick conversation. But what he *did* say was perfect…

"He wants to meet me!"

"When?"

"Today! I'm going to meet him after work – at the back entrance to Marks and Spencer!"

"Shit! What are you going to *say* to him?" Shaunna gasps.

"Um, that's what I needed to talk to you about…"

Mad, isn't it? All week, my head felt swollen, with the same question – "When's he going to call me?" – imprinted on every spare passing cell or electron or whatever it is that makes you think. Yet at no point had I figured out what I was actually going to *say* to him, all previous ideas having turned to sludge in my panicked mind. Mainly because I wasn't entirely sure whether I loved him or hated him.

Dad made it easy for me when he phoned me today, of course, by keeping the conversation so short when we spoke. But all morning, while filling all those acres of shelves, my head was throbbing with thoughts of meeting him, but again, there was no room left in my meagre, peanut-sized brain to figure out anything beyond that.

Shaunna, being Shaunna, had great advice.

"Don't say anything. Let *him* do the talking. He's supposed to be the adult here – you were barely more than a kid when he left, so let *him* do the explaining. *Then* you can talk."

And that's what I'm going to do, when he shows up. I'm

going to resist my natural urge to babble, and shut up. When he shows up…

God, I really want a cigarette, but I don't want my dad's first glimpse of me in four years to be shrouded in smoke. It's bad enough that I'm wearing my stupid uniform under my Afghan coat. I should have taken something with me to change into, but then when I left the house this morning I hadn't exactly expected to be having a reconciliation with my father by the end of the day.

If he shows up…

He did say the back entrance of M&S, didn't he? I panic, wondering if he's stuck round the front, gazing up and down the High Street, wondering where I am. But I *know* he said the back entrance – he was very particular about that. ("At the back – the set of doors nearest the multi-storey car park, yeah?" That's what he'd said.) I glance up through the pouring rain to the harshly lit levels of the car park, wondering if he's somewhere there right now, his hands shaking with nerves (like me, though the cold and damp isn't exactly helping), as he tries to lock the car door…

"Hey!" a soft voice says, at the same time as the sodden arm of my coat is squeezed.

It's on the tip of my tongue to say "Dad?", but I see that it's not him. Any other day, I'd have been ecstatic to run into Gareth outside of the club, but right at this moment it's most definitely an anticlimax.

"Oh, hi…" I mumble, though it's an effort. I think the cold has made my face muscles turn to stone.

"Are you OK? You look frozen!"

His voice is as friendly and warm as the expression in his hazel eyes. Anticlimax or not, I feel my stomach give a reflex flip of excitement.

"I'm fine," I force my mouth muscles to say, and stretch them into a smile too. "I'm waiting for my dad! He called this morning!"

Course, I'd given Gareth an update on the Dad situation last night – he'd asked me about how things were going right before Anya and co had wandered over and interrupted our conversation. It was so nice that he'd shown up right now, just at this turning-point in my life.

In fact, I hate to sound like Molly here (big fan of fate and destiny and stuff), but it's almost like it was meant to be. God, what if Dad turns up right this second? They could meet; the two men who've never been out of my thoughts lately...

"That's brilliant, Jude! What time's he coming?"

As I bend over to look at my watch, I feel the rivulets of water run off my hair, trickle down my face and drip off the end of my nose. I wish I'd taken an umbrella with me today, or that Marks and Spencer had a doorway that was deep enough to shelter in.

"Um ... he was meant to be here at five thirty," I tell Gareth, my lips trembling with cold (or something).

"But Jude – it's nearly quarter to seven! You've been waiting for more than an hour!"

Tell me something I don't know.

"He must have got held up. With the weather and everything, I mean. He lives quite a way out of town," I hear myself babbling some excuse. "I'll give it till seven..."

"Jude, you're soaked!" says Gareth with concern, getting soaked himself as he stands and talks to me. "Shouldn't you—"

My mobile starts trilling "Hey, Jude", and I find myself answering it so quickly that I don't recall actually digging it out of my bag.

"Hello?"

"Jude? It's me – it's your dad."

"It's him!" I mouth at Gareth, widening my eyes and feeling the weight of raindrops on my eyelashes.

"Great!" Gareth mouths back. "Listen – got to go!"

"Hi, Dad," I say into the phone, as I nod and smile at Gareth. He'd thrown his thumb in the direction of the junction further up the street, and when I glance that way, I see there's someone – a girl – waiting for him, standing under an umbrella. I don't recognize her at first, it's so dark and rainy, but then she moves the umbrella a fraction and in the glow of the street lamp I remember her face vaguely from the club. She must be a friend of Gareth's, maybe she goes to art school too.

"Jude, I'm so, so sorry. Something came up at the last minute and –"

I'm listening to Dad, but I'm suddenly aware that Gareth has turned back and is coming towards me.

"– I wanted to call and let you know earlier, but I could-n't get to the phone till now!"

I'm still listening, but a warm heat is radiating on my cheek from the kiss that Gareth's just planted there.

"Good luck!" he whispers, giving me a quick thumbs up before hurrying back to join his waiting friend.

"That … that's OK," I stammer down the phone.

"Listen, I can't talk now. Can I call you later, to rearrange another time?"

"Yes – um, yes, fine…"

I'm thrilled, stunned, disappointed, deliriously happy and a thousand other emotions all at once. And the clash of them all together is making me feel totally dizzy.

Or maybe the dizzy thing is just down to the fact that I've been standing here in the rain so long I've caught pneumonia...

chapter eight

Red is for danger...

Date:	*Friday 29th November*
Stressometer rating:	*Low—Medium. Trying not to get freaked out by the fact that Dad hasn't called back yet.*
Wish of the moment:	*That Dad would call back (doh).*

Helen seems to have come to her senses (in one small way) and ditched the flowery diamanté hair clips. At least, I haven't seen her wear them again this week, and since I found them lying on the bathroom floor behind the bin this morning, I think it's a case of finders-keepers.

"That's cute!" grins Gareth, tentatively reaching up and touching the two sparkly flowers I've pinned in my short hair. I have to surreptitiously bend a little to make it easier for him. Dumbo that I am, I wore my boots with the slight heel tonight. *Must* remember to always wear flat shoes around him…

"Here," I smile shyly at his compliment, and hand him a

bottle of water. "Thought you might need a drink."

It's been kind of frustrating tonight; Gareth's been bombarded with visitors up on the stage with him. Hours have passed, and this is the first chance I've had to talk to him.

"Thanks, Jude."

Gareth's eyes lock on to mine, and his fingers overlap my hand for a second longer than they need to as he takes the cold plastic bottle from my hand.

"No problem," I murmur, resisting the urge to snog him.

"Hey – I've been thinking a lot about you this week…"

This boy; he *really* knows the right things to say, doesn't he?

"Have you? Why?"

I don't actually care why, I'm just buzzing from the fact that he spent the past six days with me on his mind. Wow!

"I was wondering how things went for you – you were still on the phone to your dad when I had to go. How did it all work out?"

We're standing a hair's breadth away from each other. I love the way we have to lean in towards each other to talk, to be heard above the music. And anyway, there's not a whole lot of room up here behind the decks.

"He apologized – said something came up. He said he'd call back to rearrange another time for us to meet," I tell him, leaning myself on the lap-dance pole and then very quickly un-leaning myself.

"And?"

"And I'm still waiting," I shrug sadly.

"Hey, you know, I think it's really brilliant and really brave of you to get in touch with your dad like you did. I just hope he isn't going to disappoint you, or let you down…"

He leans away from me just enough to stare hard into my face. God, I love his concern, and I love the feeling of his hand on the small of my back…

"So," I say, feeling shy and pink under his gaze. "Who was that you were with last Saturday? When I saw you in the street?"

Gareth frowns for a second, then his fair eyebrows shoot up towards his ever-present Kangol cap as his memory kicks in.

"Last Saturday! Of course, yeah – that was Donna. You've probably seen her in here; she comes all the time."

"Ah," I nod, realizing it was just as I thought; one of his club crew.

"She's a mate. Well, she's my ex-girlfriend, actually, but we're still mates, if you see what I mean."

A jagged jolt of shock and jealousy flutters across my chest – and I hope it doesn't register on my face. 'Cause as soon as I feel it, I realize how stupid it is; Dean and Shaunna are big mates, and they dated before Dean and Molly got it together. And it's a good sign, after all. If people can be friends with their exes, then it shows how mature they are. No – I was fine with it.

"You'll have to introduce me to her sometime!" I tell him, just to show how mature and cool I am about the existence of Donna the Ex.

"Sure!" he nods, and takes a swig of the water I've brought him.

Then I see him do that slight twitch he does when he tunes into the track that's playing and knows it's time to line up the next one. Also, there's a guy hovering down on the dancefloor, right in front of the stage, looking all eager like he's desperate to make a request.

"Listen – I'll go," I tell Gareth. "Will you manage to get a break soon?"

"Nah…" he shakes his head, and checks his watch. "Too close to finishing now; I'll just work through. But come up and speak to me nearer the end, yeah?"

"Yeah…"

I wiggle my fingers at him and step off the stage, feeling his smile still boring into the back of my head.

I'll have to find Molly and Shaunna; give them the latest update on my ever-so-slowly developing thing with Gareth. At least I *hope* that's what's happening – that it's developing, I mean. I hope he doesn't just see me as yet another friend. But I don't think he does, not from the looks he gives me and the touches, never mind the tender kiss on the cheek last Saturday.

"*So?*" says Molly with meaning, as I come across her and Shaunna dancing.

"We just chatted! That's all!" I laugh.

Shaunna suddenly grabs me and gives me a big bear hug.

"Well done, Jude!" she yells in my ear. "You really have got over your addiction to creeps, haven't you? *And* your habit of snogging on the first night. That's been *four* weeks of flirting now; I tell you, waiting makes the whole thing *sooo* much better. When you two finally kiss – wow!"

She's right – only I hope I don't have *too* much longer to wait. Hasn't Shaunna ever heard of snog deprivation…?

* * *

67

Shaunna sure knows how to give a bear hug. She squashed me so hard she even smudged the make-up on my face. Yep, she's managed to make me look like I've done five rounds in the ring with Lennox Lewis – the state my mascara's in.

The only thing that's faintly safe to touch in these toilets is the water, but first you've got to turn a rusty tap on. With the tips of my fingers, I twirl the nearest tap (supposed to be hot, but runs out cold, naturally) and dampen a paper tissue in the stream.

"Scuse me…"

As I wipe the panda smear of mascara from under my right eye, I shuffle back from the sink, assuming that the auburn-haired girl beside me wants to wash her hands or something.

But she doesn't make a move towards the sink; instead, she stares hard at me, through eyes rimmed in black kohl.

"Do you want to do me a favour?" she says flatly, not a glimmer of friendliness in her eyes, not a hint of a smile on her plum-coloured lips.

"What … what do you mean?" I ask, trying to figure out what exactly's going on here. I don't *know* this girl, but I have seen her around the club before…

"Stay away from Gareth, right?" she spits out, glaring at me with a look of contempt.

"Gareth?! Why? I mean, what are you on—"

"He goes out with my friend. Is that plain enough for you?"

Is she mad?

Are we talking about the *same* Gareth?

"But—"

"That's the way it is. So leave him alone. OK?"

I'm still standing with a soggy tissue dripping water down my wrist when the red-headed girl slams the loo door on me and disappears back out into the club. And then I remember her face more clearly; one of several from the crowd, staring up at me from the dancefloor whenever I was talking to Gareth, up behind the decks.

Shit – I have to find Shaunna and Molly and tell them what's happened. I have no idea what's just gone on and I'm shaking so much that I don't think I can make sense of it on my own.

Out in the corridor, I barge past chatting boys and someone on the phone, and then feel the comforting blast of the hot, heaving dancefloor when I push open the swing door.

"Jude!" a voice calls out from somewhere, and then Adam is throwing my coat on my shoulders, grabbing me by the hand and pushing me towards the exit.

"What's going on?" I ask him, as I spot Shaunna, Molly and Dean standing chatting to Anya, of all people. I didn't even know they knew her to talk to.

"We were all looking for you!" Adam beams at me. "That girl Anya – she's having a party back at her flat right now, and she's invited us all!"

"But I … I told Gareth I'd go and speak to him again!" I try to protest, glancing back at the stage where Gareth is lost in concentration, his headphones covering his ears.

"You can speak to him next week! Anya's party sounds great, and her mate's got a minibus outside – she says we can get a lift with them if we leave right now!"

"But… But –"

I don't finish what I'm trying to say, because I can see

from my friends' beaming faces that they can't wait to go. If I had finished my sentence, I'd have said, "But I haven't said goodbye. Gareth will wonder what's happened to me…!"

As I feel myself being hustled out of the main door, I have one quick glance back in Gareth's direction. He still has his head down, nodding in time to the old Primal Scream track that's playing.

And then … you know that goosebumpy feeling you get when you know you're being watched? In fact, I suddenly remember an old wives' tale my gran once told me about – that your ears glow pink when someone's talking about you. Well, I don't know if my ears are luminous pink or not, but those two girls by the bar are *definitely* staring at me, and since their mouths are most *definitely* moving, I can only assume they're gabbing on about me too.

One is the auburn-haired witch who barked at me in the toilets two minutes ago and the other is … the girl under the umbrella from last Saturday. The girl Gareth was with. Donna – his ex, he said. But now her friend is saying they're *still* together?!

What the hell is going on?

chapter nine

Die, Barbie, die...

Date: *Friday 29th November*

Stressometer rating: *High. What's the deal with Gareth and his not-quite ex?*

Wish of the moment: *That it's all some horrible mistake...*

"Hurry up, Jude! It'll be *dawn* by the time you get out here!"

"Look, this isn't easy, you know!" I frown back at Shaunna.

I'm balancing on a rickety stool, wondering how exactly I'm going to negotiate this assault course. Since we arrived at this party I've already made a fool of myself by knocking into someone's arm and getting half a glass of red wine spilled down the front of my grey top, and having to borrow a T-shirt from Anya. (And I can't say I feel entirely comfortable wandering around with a luminous yellow T-shirt with the slogan "Die, Barbie, die!" on it.) If *that* wasn't bad enough I even managed to stand in Anya's cat's litter tray, which – at a guess – was probably last cleaned out at the turn of the millennium, probably the last time this flat in *general* was cleaned out for that matter. (By the way, it took quarter of an hour of scrubbing to get the cat poo out of the ridges in the sole of my boot – just long enough to have lots of desperate people banging on the loo door demanding to be let in.)

Honestly, I don't know how much more humiliation I can take. And that's not even starting on the weird stuff that happened back at the club with that red-headed girl…

"Hitch your skirt up!" Shaunna calls to me, bending down and sticking her head through the open half of the window.

A couple of boys standing by the rust-spotted fridge-freezer burst into catcalls at Shaunna's suggestion. I try throwing them a filthy look, but they don't seem too cowed by that. And as the only way I'm going to be able to scramble over the sink and out of the window is to do as Shaunna says, I'll just have to accept the fact that my legs are going to get gawped at.

"Come on! The view is amazing!" Molly calls through from the roof terrace (OK – the roof of the extension attached to the flat below).

"It better be…" I mumble, wriggling my long denim skirt up my thighs, so that it becomes a new-look, ruched denim mini. They'll all be copying this at the next Paris fashion shows next spring, you know…

"Here! Give me your hand!" says Shaunna, yanking me by the arm, which is more painful than helpful, since the top of my boot has caught on one of the taps and I think I'm kneeling on a fork.

God, I hate to be a moaner, but what exactly am I doing here? Not just crawling out of a window, I mean, but coming along to this party anyway? I should have let the others go on without me, and hung about to talk to Gareth, just to find out what exactly is (or isn't) going on with him and that Donna girl. Instead, I let myself be persuaded to come here via a claustrophobic ride in the back of a filthy van. Oh, yes, a *van*. Adam had been *way* over-optimistic when he'd called it a minibus; it was basically some rattling, old piece of tin on wheels that Anya's sulky boy mates used to move their band gear around in. (So *that's* what the looks of studied boredom are in aid of – Ben and Neil must fancy themselves as the next Manic Street Preachers or something.) In the end, there were ten of us and a drum kit squished in the back of the thing – we'd have looked like a bunch of drum-playing refugees being smuggled over the border if the police had stopped us.

With one final scramble and an ominous ripping sound from my fishnet tights, I find myself out in the cold night air, instantly stunned at the view of the whole of the city sprawled out sparkling in the darkness all around us.

"Great, isn't it?" says Anya, her long, tangled strands of neon hair flapping around her shoulders in the breeze. She must be freezing – all she's wearing is some baggy, orange Maharishi-type silk trousers and a black vest top.

"See? It was worth it, wasn't it?" Shaunna beams at me.

"Yes," I nod, relishing the feel of the cold, clean air in my lungs.

What I *don't* relish is the fact that as well as Anya and my friends, I'm sharing this brilliant view with the poseur double act of sour-faced Saffron (the girl I was introduced to at the club last Friday) and Neil (Mr Indie Band wannabe). I can really do without them both staring at me, even though it's understandable, since I must look like I've been dragged through a window backwards.

"Auditioning to be an Anya lookalike?" Neil says dryly, nodding his head in the direction of my borrowed dayglo T-shirt.

Wow – he really *does* think he's smart. And he really *is* deeply unfunny. I want to snap back something so cuttingly witty that he'll wish the roof terrace would open up and swallow him. Course, I don't manage to think of *anything* and so shoot him a drop-dead glare instead.

Hurray – it seems to work though, because he instantly lowers his eyes to the ground and then turns away and stares off at the view.

Nice one, Jude! I praise myself for my masterly poise and control of the situation. And then I realize that the parapet around this "roof terrace" is about five centimetres high, and I turn into a wibbly-wobbly pile of jelly. For God's sake, hasn't anyone else noticed that this flat is on the fourth floor of an old tenement block perched on a hill, which means it's a long, *long* trip to the ground?

"Are you OK? " Molly asks.

I don't know, maybe it's the fact that I've just flattened myself against the wall that gives the game away. That or the fact that my fingers are now clawing at the brickwork as the sudden rush of vertigo takes hold.

"Bit too high for me," I shrug, inching my way across the

bricks till my fingers find the safety of the window sill. "Think I'll go back in…"

Anya, Molly and Shaunna all look at me with a certain amount of disappointment but thankfully don't try and force me to stay. (Thank God Adam is inside somewhere talking to Dean and Josh and some other people from the club. If he'd been out here, I guarantee he'd have been doing a balancing act along the edge of the roof right now, just for the fun of giving everyone else heart attacks.) I don't notice what Neil or Saffron are making of my panic attack, but I'm too caught up in trying not to barf in fear that I couldn't care less if they were laughing their heads off or videoing my dilemma for *You've Been Framed*…

"See you back inside in a minute, then…" Molly calls after me, as I try to limbo dance my way back into the kitchen, folding myself into an origami emu to fit through the window and over the sink.

"Better watch out," one of the lads still leaning on the fridge leers at me. "You could catch a chill wearing a skirt so short!"

As I wrestle the rigid denim down to more discreet levels (covering the gaping hole the fork tore in the knee of my fishnets), I find myself wishing my friends would follow me in right now; not just to outnumber the drongos who are teasing me, but to give me a chance to talk to them about what happened back at the club. It's just that I haven't had a chance to tell them what went on: first, we ended up playing the sardine game in the back of the van (*not* a great way to guarantee privacy) and ever since we arrived at her flat, Anya's been acting like our new best friend. Any other time I'd love a chance to hang out with her – her flat is amazing, if messy – but I'd give anything to have Molly and Shaunna to myself right now, so I can talk to them about the potential Donna disaster...

And then I see something that makes my heart beat as crazily as if I were perched on the non-existent ledge outside the kitchen window. It's not the sight of the silver-sprayed walls or the vast, unframed pink and purple abstract paintings stuck on them – I already had my eyeballs seared by that when we arrived, as well as by the vision of poodle-pink fun-fur fabric covering every seat and sofa in the place (including the rickety stool I'd been perching on five minutes ago).

Nope, this particular vision isn't pink or purple or silver or furry, unless of course you count his skin as a pale shade of pink and the fluffy edging on his parka hood as fur...

Omigod ... I quickly try and unroll the last stubborn creases of denim in my skirt so I don't look like a complete half-dressed doughball when Gareth comes over. 'Cause that's where he's headed – in the direction of *me*.

"Brilliant! I didn't know you were going to be here, Jude!"

That's got to be a good sign, hasn't it? Would he be so pleased to see me if he was going out with someone else? And wouldn't he have brought that Donna girl with him tonight, if they were an item?

"I didn't know I was going to be here either!" I try to joke, while my mind whirrs at the speed of light. "I was kidnapped by my friends!"

Wait a minute, here's another thing – wouldn't I have seen Gareth and Donna hanging out with each other more at the club if they were dating? That red-headed girl *has* to be making the whole thing up. More than anything, I want to talk to Gareth about what she said, but I'll have to do it really subtly, so I don't come over like some clingy, love-hungry stalker…

"You, know, I was *wondering* why you didn't say good-bye."

His eyes are twinkling; his voice is soft and suggestive. He's teasing me, in that flirty sort of way you just don't use when you've got a girlfriend tucked away. I *hope*.

"Well, I *meant* to," I tell him, hoping I don't sound too obvious.

"Like the T-shirt, by the way. It's one of Anya's, right?"

It's a simple observation, without a trace of the sarcasm that Neil had snarled my way a few minutes ago. Actually, from the flattering way Gareth is checking me out, I'd almost say dayglo yellow is going to be my new favourite colour.

"Yeah, it's Anya's," I nod. "Someone spilt red wine on my top and I had to borrow this from her."

"No – I mean it's one of her own designs," Gareth elaborates. "She does those at art school, and she sells them on her own label on a stall at Exham Street Market on Saturdays."

Does she? Wow – Exham Street Market is like our city's version of Camden Market. Very hip, very happening – if that doesn't sound too much like the sort of expression Helen would come out with.

"It's … it's great," I try to say with enthusiasm, holding out the T-shirt by the hem and studying it upside-down.

"Yeah, she's a bit of a star, our Anya. The next Tracey Emin."

Tracey Emin … ditzy British artist who's famous for building messy versions of her bedroom in art galleries. Maybe Anya should give up the slogan T-shirts and just enter her cat's minging litter tray for the next Turner Prize and she'll be laughing all the way to the bank. Maybe she'll even earn enough to get a cleaner…

This isn't getting us anywhere. Mention the club. If you start talking about that, you can gradually, casually work your way round to the one-way conversation you had with the red-headed girl, I tell myself.

"You know when I came up and saw you? When I gave you that bottle of water?" I say out loud, not really sure where I'm going to steer this.

"Yeah," Gareth nods, shirking his parka off his shoulders.

"Well … after that, I went to the loo and this girl came up to me and told me you were still going out with Donna."

Mmm … nice one, Jude! *Really* subtle! *Really* casual! Why don't you just open your big gob and say the first thing that pops into your mind without actually thinking about it? Oh, you already have…

"Uh … *who* said that, exactly?" Gareth frowns in confusion, pushing his cap further back on his forehead with one hand.

"A girl."

Doh, Jude. You've started now so you might as well finish.

"A girl with long, straight auburn hair. And dark lipstick. And I saw her talking to Donna right before I left the club."

"That'll be Lisa!" Gareth sighs, like he's heard this all before. "Jeez, Jude – don't worry about her!"

"No?" I whisper, wide-eyed, instantly wondering if I shouldn't have played it cooler and muttered something offhand like, "Hey, who said anything about that girl worrying me?"

"She's this old friend of Donna's –" Gareth bats his long, sandy eyelashes at me – "and she's got this mad idea that me and Donna should get back together. But that's not the way me and Donna feel about it, honest!"

His eyes are begging me to understand. Or am I just fooling myself?

"Honest?" I hear myself asking in a truly pathetic tone of voice.

"Honest," Gareth repeats with a soft, spine-dissolving smile. "Trust me, Jude, there's no *way* Donna and I would ever get back together."

"Why not?" I ask in a high-pitched Barbie doll squeak. (And *this* Barbie is going to "Die, Barbie, die" from pure stress the way my heart is thundering.)

But Gareth doesn't bother to answer me. Not because he doesn't give a damn, because he so clearly *does* judging from the way he's suddenly kissing me…

Shaunna's right, you know. Waiting this long is *so* worth it…

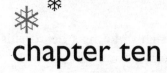

chapter ten

How to make me feel that _small_

Date: _Sunday 1st December_

Stressometer rating: _Medium(ish). Busy waiting for a phone that never rings._

Wish of the moment: _Ring, damn you!_

"THE BABY BROTHER I NEVER KNEW I HAD!"

Tell me about it, I think, as I stare at the headline in the Sunday paper. Of course, I'm not quite as ancient as the woman in this feature, who's about 80, while her "baby" brother's definitely collecting-his-pension age. And I don't know for _sure_ that I have a baby brother (or sister), but I suppose it's a 99% dead cert. Still, reading this is a bit of a sharp reminder of the black cloud that I've been trying to ignore, i.e. the fact that my mobile phone is staying so resolutely quiet.

It's just that now I've got _two_ people who aren't ringing me: Dad _and_ Gareth. Dad ... well, I don't know what complications he's got going on in his life these days. And as for Gareth … oh, please, please, *please* don't let me have got it wrong where he's concerned. *Please* let him be a good guy. But if he *is* a good guy, why hasn't he phoned me like he promised he would? I know it's only been a couple of days, but everything changed with that kiss. Didn't it?

My brain has been going around in so many circles that if I think about all that for one second longer it might just pack up on me through sheer exhaustion. Quick: I should distract myself. I flick to the next page of my magazine, and the next, and the next, my still-sleepy eyes skimming over stories of vaguely famous people doing outrageous things like wearing something crap to a premiere or putting a bag of rubbish outside their house without any make-up on. Normally I like reading entertaining drivel like this on a Sunday morning, as I come to with a cup of coffee or three and a mountain of toast. It's part of my routine, along with watching *T4* on the portable TV, while Helen snoozes away the morning like the teenager she thinks she is. But today, I can't concentrate, not with my half-awake head clogged up with thoughts of Friday night and that kiss (and the others that followed it)…

How to make a lovely memory evaporate into thin air: listen to the sound of a toilet flushing.

"Great," I mumble to myself grumpily.

Helen's up much earlier than usual, so bang goes my precious Sunday morning ritual. She'll be down any minute now, yawning like a seal on heat, cluttering up the kitchen with all her noise and mess and the sickening smell of porridge she likes so much. (How can anyone eat anything that smells so toxic?)

I check the kitchen clock and see that it's just gone 9.30 a.m. – what is she doing up so early, considering I heard her clattering her way into the house at around two o'clock last night? Wherever she'd been, she must have had fun (and gallons to drink), considering I heard her giggling to herself as she creaked her way noisily up the stairs to her room…

"Uh, hello…!"

I jump at the sound of a voice I don't recognize, spilling a trail of toast crumbs over the *News of the World*.

Good grief. There is a guy standing in the doorway of my kitchen wearing nothing but a faded pair of Levi's, which are halfway undone and revealing slightly more abdomen than I'm used to seeing.

"Jude, isn't it?" he yawns contentedly, while scratching his messy mop of hair.

"Um … yes," I reply dubiously.

This is the toy-boy I saw Helen snogging in our living room two weeks ago. My God, he's stayed the night. So that's why she was giggling on the way up the stairs in the early hours…

"Wow, that coffee smells good. Where do you keep it?"

I point in the direction of the kettle and the tray of coffee, tea-bags and sugar that lives beside it and marvel at how relaxed and casual this stranger feels as he pads across the kitchen semi-naked.

And excuse me, but I also marvel at the cheek of Helen for inviting this person back without letting me know. I mean, I could have been in the shower (OK, so I almost always lock the door), or sitting here in the kitchen in just my undies (OK, so I've never done that).

But the main thing is ... well ... omigod, the idea of my mother actually *sleeping* with someone in the next room to me! Aargh! I don't care what she gets up to when she goes out, but to bring a guy back here... The very thought of it is making me cringe to the soles of my Birkenstocks.

"Where do you keep the mugs?"

Luckily, I hear my mobile ringing in my bag out in the hall, and make a leap for it before I can help this bloke feel any more at home in our house than he apparently already does.

"Hello?" I say, clamping the phone to my head without checking whose number is calling and leaning one hand against the hallway wall.

Please, *please* let this be Gareth.

"Jude?"

Or my dad.

"Hi ... there," I greet him, finding it too weird to call him "Dad" out loud, since he hasn't exactly *earned* that title any time lately.

And just as well I didn't say it out loud – here comes Helen, padding down the stairs with messed-up bed-head hair, and dressed in her favourite over-sized, holey jumper and a pair of boxer shorts. (Oh, please don't let those be *his* boxer shorts. That would just be way too cosy, not to mention unhygienic...)

"Morning!" she whispers at me, having the cheek to smile and look not the least bit embarrassed.

"Jude, I'm so sorry it's taken me so long to get back to you," I hear my dad say. "It's just that it's been another mad week."

"That's OK," I tell him, as I watch Helen meander into the kitchen.

If she only knew…

"Listen, I can't really talk right now –"

I am listening to what he's saying – of course I am – but I can't help taking a step to the left and peering in to the kitchen. And what a sight to behold; my mother and a guy who must be practically young enough to be her son, gazing slushily into each other's eyes, arms wrapped round each other's waists.

"Who's that?" Helen suddenly turns and mouths at me, somehow sensing that I'm watching. (I'd call it mother's intuition, only Helen kind of gave up on being a mother a long time ago.)

"Molly," I mouth back my white lie.

"– but I just thought maybe we could meet on Tuesday after you get out of school? Maybe at that café by the bus station, at five-ish?"

Helen's let go of her toy-boy and is now sorting out the mugs and the coffee for them both.

"Yeah, no problem," I reply, hoping I sound a million times calmer than I feel.

"Great. Well, I'd better go. See you then, Jude. Bye!"

Omigod, Toy-Boy has just playfully smacked Helen on the bum, and she's giggling like a fool. I think I may gag.

"Bye…"

You know something? Suddenly, it feels quite good to have such a huge secret that Helen knows nothing about…

"I've got to go…"

"Don't go, Jude."

That's what Gareth had said to me, with such begging, puppy-dog eyes that I practically turned to melted toffee inside.

"I've got to … I'm sharing a cab with my friends!"

"Get a cab later."

"I can't!" I'd smiled at him ruefully, untangling myself from his arms and reluctantly getting up from the sofa.

"Give me your number, then – I'll call you tomorrow."

"OK." I'd giggled, pulling out a pen and a scrap of paper from my bag and scribbling furiously. "But remember I'll be working tomorrow during the day."

"Well, I'll call you at night. Or I'll text you during the day. Or I'll send a white dove to Tesco's with a message for you tied around its leg…"

And I'd giggled again, not believing my luck. I certainly didn't believe my (terrible) luck when the whole of the following day (yesterday) sped by without a call, without a text, without so much as a dove…

"Jude, here's a tip: think before you just go rushing in and do stuff."

That's one of Shaunna's gems. It's the sort of thing that she's come out with in the past when I've spent exactly five seconds deciding I have a monumental crush on someone who turns out in the end to be a real turkey. Or when I do dumb things in general, like spend my entire month's wages on a pair of ridiculously high, ridiculously strappy shoes that end up being worn exactly once, around my bedroom; or get a whim to paint my bedroom pillar-box red one weekend and end up having to paint it cream the next weekend after seven days' worth of migraines.

But the way I see it, if I don't dive in and give things a

go, I'll just let the thought fester in my mind, working myself into a tizz and then bottling it.

Like now: if I'd seriously thought about what I was doing, I wouldn't have tramped across town in a semi-blizzard, and found myself knocking on Anya's door this Sunday afternoon. It's just that she's the only person I know who might have Gareth's phone number, and calling him – I've decided – is the only way I can find out why he hasn't called me. (And it sure beats staying at home watching Helen and her toy-boy feeding each other bits of *croissant*, for God's sake.)

I know Shaunna and Molly would have a fit if they knew what I was doing (which is why I haven't told them), but they wouldn't have to worry. I'll think up some excuse for phoning Gareth, just so he doesn't feel I'm hassling him, or coming on too strong. I just haven't quite worked out what that's going to be yet...

"Hey! It's..."

"Jude!" I helpfully fill in the gap when Anya – dressed in cosy socks, cosy tracksuit bottoms and an even cosier fleece or three – pulls open her front door with a rattle of bracelets.

"Jude! Of course! Sorry – I haven't really woken up yet!"

Anya, make-up free and with her extensions dragged back into a messy ponytail, stands to one side and ushers me in.

Urgh ... this girl might be warm and welcoming, but her flat by daylight certainly isn't. The amazing silver-sprayed walls look tacky and patchy, and even her huge artworks seem more primary school than art school now. The temperature in here is about two degrees warmer than it is outside, so it's no wonder that as soon as Anya leads the way back to the living room, she dives under a crumpled old duvet she must have dragged through from her bedroom. She's sharing it, I see, with a scruffy ginger cat that must be the proud owner of the litter tray I stood in the other night. The only other source of heat that I can see is a tiny, old-fashioned two-bar electric fire which is positioned close to the beer-can-strewn coffee table. Is that still left-overs from Friday night, or was there more partying going on here last night? Still, you can't blame Anya for inviting people round – generating a lot of body heat is probably the only way she ever gets this flat above freezing.

"Have a seat!" says Anya, gesturing to a grubby armchair before snuggling her arm under the duvet. "I'd offer you a tea, only I've run out of milk. And tea. But Neil and Ben have nipped out to Spar at the end of the street, so they should be back with stuff any second…"

"That's … that's nice of them," I mumble, trying to work out what exactly the relationship is between Anya and her two moody mates. Are they flatmates too? I don't think I spotted more than one bedroom when I was here on Friday…

"Oh, it's not nice of them. I told them they *had* to, since I let them crash here last night. They didn't fancy walking home to their own place in the snow, but I haven't managed to get rid of them yet, so I thought they might as well make themselves useful."

I'd have thought that guy Neil would have had his rubbish, rusty van to drive home in but then I think, judging by the pile of beer-cans kicking about, he probably wasn't in any state to be driving. Still, if I were him or Ben, I think I might have preferred a sub-zero walk home than risk waking up with frostbite in this igloo of a flat.

"So, what brings you round here, Jude?"

Anya yawns, and then unself-consciously wrinkles her nose above the musty-looking duvet as she speaks, reminding me of the sleepy dormouse at the Mad Hatter's tea party. (With a snoring Cheshire Cat beside her.) And she's a technicolour dormouse of course, which is more than mad enough for a Mad Hatter's tea party, I guess.

"Just came to give you back the top you lent me," I shrug, holding out a plastic bag with her "Die, Barbie, die" T-shirt.

"You didn't have to do that! You could have given it to me next Friday at the club!"

I know that. I hope she doesn't spot it for the pathetic excuse it is.

"I just wondered," I carry on regardless, "whether you had Gareth – Gareth from the club – whether you had his phone number. Or not. I just really need … I mean, I *want* to speak to him."

Wow, that must have sounded very cool. Not at all desperate or anything. I don't think.

"Gareth…?" Anya frowns and wrinkles her dormouse nose again. "Um, I'm not sure if I do. I mean, I think I might have had it once, but I can't think where I'd have written it down. Oh, hold on!"

There's a clatter as the front door bursts open and then the cackle and laughter of boys. Which stops dead when Neil and Ben walk in the room – shedding snowflakes – and see me sitting there. What's their problem? Don't they like to share their friend or something?

"Hope you brought me a present!" Anya grins at them, eyeing up the bulging plastic bag Ben's carrying.

Neil and Ben – they look practically identical in their trendy, nylon kagoule-style jackets, jeans, beat-up Vans trainers and deliberately scruffy hairdos.

"Let's see: milk … rolls … tea-bags…" Ben intones, his shaggy head of hair bent over the bag. "And Jaffa Cakes, of *course*…"

He tosses the packet of biscuits through the air, and Anya slips her arms out of her duvet burrow at lightning speed and catches them with a surprised giggle.

Neil, meanwhile, seems to be studying my gloves with an expression of stupefied distaste. OK, so they're mittens, but I thought they were cute when I bought them, together with this matching tassle-ended scarf, in TopShop. They're in fashion! Anyway, has he *seen* what the weather's doing out there? Oh, God, he's thinks I'm about three years old, doesn't he…

"Oh, Neil – Jude's here 'cause she was trying to get a number for Gareth," Anya suddenly jumps in, like she's remembered my existence after being momentarily distracted by biscuits and whooping. "You've got his number, haven't you?"

I'm busy shaking my head at the newly opened packet that Anya's holding out to me, but I look around at the boys quickly enough to catch the tail-end of a knowing stare. Why are they doing that? It's so mortifying! Do they think I'm too young for him? Or am I just not cool enough for their friend to be seen with, me with my mittens and schoolgirl crush?

God, I wish I hadn't come here today...

"Yeah, wait a minute," Neil mumbles, tearing his mocking gaze away from Ben just long enough to pull out a mobile.

I yank off my mittens quickly, grab my own mobile and key in the number that Neil's now reciting from his mobile's screen. Ben, meanwhile is sniggering and I don't understand what at. Then Anya makes it clear.

"*Neil!* That's not Gareth's number! That's the number of the Pizza Hut on Prince Street. I called it the other night, you idiot!"

"Um, sorry ... my mistake," Neil smiles wickedly and shrugs. "Here – this is the right one".

Thanks to Neil's attempt to humiliate me, I feel my face burning as I delete and re-enter the correct number.

"You can be *such* an idiot, Neil," I hear Anya say. At least what he's told me must be the real thing this time, since she's not contradicting him.

"Thanks – I'd better be going," I say to Anya – deliberately ignoring Neil and Ben – as I gather myself together to go. (Mittens: check. Mobile: check. Pride: long gone...)

"Aw ... are you sure? You don't want to stay for a cup of tea or something?" asks Anya, following me out with her duvet wrapped around her like an over-stuffed security blanket.

Just to show I'm not as childish as them, I manage what I hope looks like a casual nod in the direction of Ben and Neil as I shuffle past them. Knowing me, it probably comes across more like a nervous tic.

"No, but thanks," I tell Anya, as she pulls the front door open. "Got stuff to do..."

"Like chase after Gareth!" I hear Ben snickering back in the living room.

From her eyes, I can tell Anya's heard that too, but she's smiling at me and waving as I make my wobbly way down the stairs, hoping – I guess – that I missed that snidey bit of bitching.

As soon as I step out into the street, I'm enveloped in a whirl of thick snow; so thick that I can hardly tell the pavement from the street. But I like the sensation; after burning up with shame just now, the biting coldness and pure, white snow is like a cold flannel on a feverish forehead.

Those obnoxious lads... How dare they make me feel like that? After all, I've done enough running after bad boys in my time. Surely there's no harm in running after a good guy for a change...?

chapter eleven

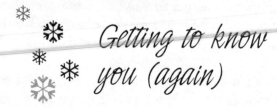

Getting to know
you (again)

Date: *Tuesday 3rd December*

Stressometer rating: *High. This is D-Day: Dad day...*

Wish of the moment: *That I don't get stood up again.*

"So…"

Helen has her head down over some books spread out on the kitchen table – homework, I guess. Still, homework or not, she appears to be about to start a conversation which, I'm sorry, but I just don't have time for. I'm about to go on a hot date – well, not a hot date exactly, since Gareth hasn't got back to the couple of messages I left on his answer service. But it's a VIM (Very Important Meeting) all the same.

"Have you seen the iron?" I demand, aware that I'm asking a stupid question. It's probably in the recycling bin, knowing Helen.

Look at the time … it's 4.30 p.m. already. I need to iron my grey trousers and get out of here in the next few minutes to make it to the bus station café for five o'clock.

"Isn't it in the cupboard?" she raises her head and asks.

"*No*. It's not in the cupboard where it *should* be."

"Oh. Well, maybe I left it in my room…"

Stuff it. I don't have time to mount a search party – I'll wear my jeans instead. Anything as long as it's not my stupid school uniform (now languishing in a pile on my bedroom floor, while I run around in my new fleece, knickers and socks).

"So, anyway, Jude – I meant to ask you, what do you think of Will?"

I look at Helen blankly. I have a feeling she's talking about Toy-Boy here, but frankly, I don't feel like making things easier for her. And she's also annoying me by wearing some new T-shirt that says "Babe" on the front in some swirly '70s-style print. Good grief – is she going to end up coming home at some point with one of Anya's designs from Exham Market? And another thing: I'm not in the mood to have some bonding girlie chat about her new boyfriend or whatever he is, when mine (or whatever he is) hasn't bothered returning the message I left on his mobile on Sunday. Or the one I left on Monday. Or the one I left this morning…

"Will," Helen repeats, with a slight twitch at the corner of her mouth, as if she's feeling a little self-conscious or embarrassed. And so she should be; she has some ridiculously young bloke stay the night, acts like nothing's happened for the last few days, then suddenly decides she wants to talk about it? I don't *think* so…

"Will?" I frown at her, deliberately pretending not to understand who she's on about, as I rifle in the laundry basket for my jeans and start pulling them on.

"Will. You met him on Sunday. And you've seen him here before, when I've had friends around."

I could have pointed out that I don't pay much attention to her friends, or said something cutting about Will being so young that from what I've seen of him, he doesn't seem to be able to dress himself in the mornings without the help of his mummy. But I don't want to seem petty.

"Oh, him. What about him?"

Helen tucks one side of her hair agitatedly behind her ear. Could she be losing her patience a little bit? Good.

"I *said*, what do you think of him?"

"Dunno, really," I mumble, slipping my feet into my boots. "Listen, I've got to go. I'm late for something."

And since Helen is more interested in her own life and doesn't even bother asking where I'm going, I feel absolutely fine about keeping the secret of Dad to myself for now…

Expensive khaki trousers, silky-knit V-neck jersey, black wool overcoat. Oh, and the same short, slicked-back hair he's always had, only now slightly greying at the edges and rigid with some kind of gel or something. (Must be *her* influence…)

"My God, Jude! You look so … so different!"

It's a pretty dumb thing to say – last time I saw Dad I was younger, shorter, spottier, pudgier, had a style-less hair-style and got sad crushes on anyone who happened to be number one in the charts. If I *wasn't* different, then there'd be something majorly wrong with me.

Still, it's taking all of my will power to stop myself from crying. He's the git who walked out on us (without sticking around to see the changes that got me here), and who's got a whole new family that he's never bothered letting us know about. But then again, he's still my dad…

He's staring at me from the opposite side of the scuzzy formica table, taking in every detail of my face as if he was a 19th century anthropologist studying the Elephant Man.

"Ah, Jude, Jude, Jude…" Dad mutters, gazing at me in awe.

I wish I'd got up when he first walked in here; maybe we wouldn't have felt so awkward; maybe we could have hugged, kissed, even. And I wish our first meeting hadn't been in this café that's grottier than I'd ever expected it to be from the few times I'd peered in when I was passing. Half the customers are reluctantly sheltering in here out of the cold, while they wait for their buses; the other half make it look like this is the hip meeting place for all the low-life within a ten-kilometre radius. The bloke in the booth by the door; I *swear* he smelled of wee when I first passed him on the way in here…

"Like the piercing, Jude. Very trendy," Dad comments, making me relax enough to manage a wavery smile.

Then I bite my lip and fidget with the furry-edged sleeve of my Afghan coat. Shaunna drummed it into me again today; let *him* do the talking at first. And that's exactly what I was going to do.

"Well … it's been too long, hasn't it?"

I nod at his statement, feeling a snap of recognition as I

study his features. Before, he was just … *Dad*, but now I see that with his dark, cropped hair, those brown eyes, that nose and cheekbones and smile … it's a male version of what I see in the mirror every day. My God, I'm so much more like him than Helen, and I didn't even realize it till now.

"And I can't stay long, Jude … not today. I've got to pick up Maggie from her sister's soon."

"Maggie? Is that her name? Your girlfriend, I mean?" I hear myself blurt out, curiosity getting in the way of my cunning plan to stay silent and force more grovelling out of him.

"Yes."

Dad lowers his head down and studies his clasped hands. He looks like a naughty little schoolboy who's been caught putting soap powder in the goldfish pond, not a grown man of 40 with a successful career as a freelance architect and two – count 'em; *two* – families. Which brings me on to…

"And what about the baby?" I ask outright. (Sorry, Shaunna, I'm not sticking by your rules at all.)

"Oliver?" he squeaks, as much as a 40-something-year-old guy can squeak. "How did you know about Oliver?"

A baby brother. I have a baby brother. Well, that answers *one* question, then.

But I don't know if I can answer *Dad's* question; confessing to being this loser who scrabbles around in bushes, spying on him. So I decide to lie.

"Just a guess. I mean, you've been with … with Maggie four years now. Chances are you'd have a kid together."

I nearly choked on the word "kid", but I just got away with it without cracking up.

Dad's fingers are trembling as he reaches into his inside coat pocket. He pulls out his wallet, and flips it open to show me a photo he keeps in there. (It's all so familiar. I remember a different wallet, and a picture of Helen and a small version of me in there.)

My eyes scan the snap; Maggie is petite and blonde and curvy and perfect. Her hair looks expensively cut, her make-up is immaculate, and the cute, blond baby on her lap is dressed in groovy Baby Gap denim and fleece. Me and Helen, we look like a couple of malnourished crusties next to these two. Dad's angelic family versus the skinny, scruff-buckets he left behind…

"That was taken on Oliver's first birthday a couple of months ago. The 23rd of October."

Funny; mine was exactly a month earlier – the 23rd of September. Funnier still that Dad seems to have conveniently forgotten that.

"Why did you leave me and Helen the way you did, so suddenly?" I ask bluntly, now that fact of forgotten birthdays has pricked the bubble of euphoria I've been feeling.

"Helen?" Dad frowns.

"Mum, then." I shrug, not really ready to explain away all the changes that have happened over the last few years before he gives me *his* explanations.

"Because … because I was very sure that I had to leave, and I knew your mother all too well," he says sorrowfully.

"Meaning?"

I'm challenging him, and I feel shaky for doing it. I'm peanut-brain Jude, prize worrier and champion panicker, but here I am taking on my father. Who knew?

"I was sure I loved Maggie. And I knew that your mother

was so ... so ... I'm sorry, Jude, but because your mother was always so clingy I thought she'd *never* be able to let go."

Helen? Clingy? She's certainly not that now (not by a long, long shot), and I can't even remember her being like that in any way when the three of us were together.

It's like Dad can read my mind. Spooky.

"You were only young, Jude. Remember, me and your mum had a lot of years together, before you were born and when you were too young to appreciate how things were between us. She was very possessive, your mother. It caused a lot of problems. And I knew that if I tried – much as I wanted to – to split amicably, and to stay in touch, it just wouldn't work."

I blink at him, trying to absorb this idea of a Helen I've never seen.

"And so, after weeks of agonizing," he continues, playing absently with the sugar cubes on the saucer of his coffee cup, "I decided that the kindest thing to do was cut off altogether. A clean break. It's the only way I could see it working with your mother – not dragging things on. Though it broke my heart knowing that I couldn't see you... But my own feelings weren't important. All that mattered was knowing you'd be safe and cared for by your mum. She loves you a lot, I know it..."

I don't, but Dad doesn't know that. Oh, damn – I'm going to cry and I was trying so hard not to.

"It's nothing to do with how I felt about you, Jude!" says Dad, handing me a scratchy napkin out of the dispenser. "It's me who suffered in all this, having to leave you behind, but I knew it was the best thing for you."

"And your baby? Oliver? Why didn't you tell –"

I can't quite finish because my throat is seizing up.

"Jude – me and your mother have only spoken on the phone three times since we broke up, and those three times were all very short and brusque, all to do with financial arrangements. I don't think she'd have really appreciated me calling up with the glad tidings. It would have been like rubbing her nose in it."

I guess I could see where he was coming from, even if I couldn't actually say so, since the lump in my throat was making talking an impossibility.

"Listen, Jude – I'm sorry, but I really am going to have to run," says Dad, looking worriedly at his watch. "But why don't I call you later, and we can arrange to spend the afternoon together sometime soon? Sometime before Christmas?"

"Yes, I'd like that," I whisper, trying to dab the worst of the snot from my runny nose (which has come out in sympathy with my eyes) just in case Dad wants to kiss me goodbye.

"I'm so happy we're back in touch, Jude..." he tells me as he stands up, then bends and plants a kiss on the top of my head, just like he used to do when he came into my room in the evenings to say goodnight.

"So am I," I blink up at him as he begins to walk away, still smiling warmly at me over his shoulder.

"Oh, and Jude –"

He's hesitated, two steps away from me.

"– you won't tell your mum about this, will you? I think it would upset her too much..."

"No, of course not," I reply, shutting my eyes for emphasis as I shake my head. And when I open them a millisecond later, he's gone, his long black coat a blur in the rain-splattered window of the café.

There're still a million questions I need to ask him, a million gaps that need to be filled. But for now, I've got my dad back in my life and that's the best (early) Christmas present I could ever hope for.

Course, I wouldn't say no to being Gareth's girlfriend either. (Is that asking Santa too much…?)

chapter twelve

Wrong place, wrong party

Date:	*Friday 6th December*
Stressometer rating:	*High. Three calls to Gareth; zero replies.*
Wish of the moment:	*I wish I wasn't at this party...*

The tune that's playing when me and Shaunna walk in – I can't quite remember what it is; some novelty song that got to number one a couple of years ago. Whatever it is, it's awful.

"Come on – *daaannccce!*"

It's Friday night, and Gareth is behind the decks, sorting out the records he'll be playing as the evening wears on. It's still early, but the club is already buzzing with people. God, I wish I was there ... instead of stuck here in a glorified Scout Hall with all of Dean's relatives, both elderly and small.

"Please, *please* dance with me!"

"Not yet, Bethany, sweetheart. Me and Jude have only just got here," says Shaunna to the four year old dressed as the Little Mermaid, who's currently trying to drag my friend by the knees to the so-called dancefloor of this over-sized shed. "We've got to give your cousin Dean his birthday presents, haven't we?"

The Little Mermaid looks momentarily sulky, then hoists up her flowing green skirts and skips off in her rain-bow-coloured wellies.

"She's still into them, then?" I point after Bethany.

Bethany is Adam's niece, his sister Lynsey's kid. Adam's older brother Brian married Shaunna's older sister Ruth earlier this year. I mention this complicated family tangle only 'cause Bethany caused quite a stir at their wedding by refusing to be a flower girl unless she got to wear her wellies.

"Yep," Shaunna nods. "They're her 'party' shoes, apparently. Wonder if they'll catch on for the over-fives? Maybe we'll go the club next Friday night and see Anya strutting her stuff in a pair of them. She'd quite suit them!"

Next Friday night ... that's *way* too far away. I want to see Gareth tonight, to find out why he's never returned my calls, why he hasn't wanted an action replay of those kisses we shared. I'm getting myself seriously stressed-out by this. I can't figure out whether I'm hurt and disap-pointed or just plain mad at him. But before I go losing faith in Gareth, I need to give him the chance to explain himself, and the sooner the better. But I can hardly blow out Dean's 18th birthday party, can I? Not when half of the people who normally go to the club are here helping Dean celebrate. At least, a whole chunk of Dean's friends from his sixth-form college, like Josh, and loads of other people I now know to say hi to. And thank God they *are* here, since Dean's been a bit over-zealous with his party invites to the aunt and uncle/granny and grandad brigade. There are about three long tables full of assorted relatives, who'll all probably be keeping an eye out for under-age drinkers. (Good grief, now it feels like a proper Scout meeting in a Scout Hall, despite all the balloons and dodgy disco lights.)

"And why did Dean want to have his party here?" I ask Shaunna, as I shake off my coat.

There are plenty of great venues he could have chosen. Like the Kennington Hotel down the road – loads of people from school have their 16ths or 18ths there, and it's got an amazing room with a balcony overlooking the river. Or he could have ditched the oldsters and just spent his birthday with all his friends down at "Loaded" tonight... I *wish*.

"His Auntie Anne runs the local Weight Watchers' club here, apparently," Shaunna explains. "She got the hire of it cheap and said she'd treat him to it as a birthday present."

"And Dean was too polite to refuse?" I suggest.

"Yep. That's what Molly said."

Speak of the devils. There's the birthday boy on the far side of the room, being presented with zillions of parcels by Molly.

"Hey, exactly how many presents did Molly buy Dean?" I whisper to Shaunna, glancing down at my own weedy effort. One "Chill-Out" compilation CD seems like peanuts compared to the mound of birthday gifts that Molly is laying at her beloved's feet. Well, near enough...

"I think she's auditioning for the role of Santa Claus," Shaunna replies, gazing over at Dean, who is now doing a catalogue model pose in his new jacket. "Only she's forgotten that the gifts are meant to be spread out amongst everyone in the world, not just given to one person."

"How can she afford it?" I frown.

"Maybe she sold her house behind her parents' backs?"

Hmm. Molly's parents are looking blissfully ignorant at the moment, so who knows? They're sitting on the same table as Dean's mum and dad, like they're doing a dress rehearsal for being at a wedding reception sometime in the future... How weird.

"Hey, look – Bethany's found herself a dancing partner!"

I check where Shaunna's pointing and see Adam bouncing between the tables with a squealing Bethany on his shoulders.

Very cute. But I don't want to be at a cosy kiddy party with grannies getting up to do "The Birdie Song". I want to be down at the club, where the adults are, where Gareth is...

"By the way, what did you guys get Dean?" I ask Shaunna, trying to throw off the blues and act a little enthusiastic. (Hard. *Very* hard.)

"Urgh... It was Adam's choice," Shaunna says, rolling her eyes. "It's this desk-top mobile-phone-holder thing in the shape of a skull. Its eye sockets flash red when you put the phone in. Hey, you'll probably get a look at it later – Adam will be *dying* to show it off to everyone..."

Wow. Corny music, a venue with all the ambience of a garden shed, kids and grannies running riot and the potential of a flashing plastic skull to play with. This night was just getting more and more exciting.

Not.

I didn't realize that Shaunna's mum and dad had been invited too, but there they are, dancing to Shaggy's "Boombastic", of all things, with Molly's folks. All we need now is for Helen to show up and we'll have a regular parents' night.

Anyway, what's with the ropey music? Dean promised earlier that this kind of stuff would only be on for a while to keep the oldsters and the little kids happy, and then the decent music would kick in. Well, I'm still waiting...

I'm on my own at the moment, sipping on flat Coke and pushing aside my uneaten piece of birthday cake, while Molly and Shaunna have got themselves into the spirit of things and are currently spinning around the dancefloor with Bethany, and Molly's little sister Mia.

God, I'm *so* annoyed with myself; why can't I be a better actress (and a better friend) and pretend like I'm having fun? Because my heart is being ripped in two with uncertainty, *that's* why. I can't sit here and make out everything is great when, more than anything, all I want is to be on the other side of town, finding out if I've got the faintest chance of a future with Gareth.

Oh no... Now Adam's started a conga line, grabbing his and Dean's grandmother by her ample waist and pushing her though the crowd. Everyone's grabbing hold of everyone. It's going to be a matter of seconds before he leaves the dancefloor and starts recruiting from the tables. I can't do this... I just can't do this. I just don't have the emotional energy to fake having fun.

While everyone is laughing and looking the other way, I make a scramble for my bag and coat and leg it to the door. But before I hurry out into the cold December night, I nip to the Ladies loos and scribble a message on the mirror in lipstick: "Shaunna, Molly – so sorry, have to go. Got to see Gareth!"

I sign off with my name and some kisses, in the vain hope that the kisses will win me a few points with my friends.

I know they're going to be so mad with me, but hey, sometimes you've got to do what your heart says, even if you don't exactly understand what it's trying to tell you...

chapter thirteen

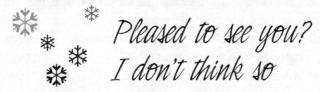

Pleased to see you?
I don't think so

Date:	*Friday 6th December*
Stressometer rating:	*High. Who does Helen think she is?*
Wish of the moment:	*That I'd never been born.*

"Hey, doll-face – what's the rush?"

Some guy's beery breath accosts me as I try to squeeze past him and his buddies, all standing clogging up the corridor leading into the club.

The rush is to get away from your toxic breath, I think to myself, as I blank him, and attempt to push away the hand of his that's on my waist right this second, trying to stop me from getting anywhere.

"C'mon, babe… Don't I get a little smile?"

I've got on my boots with the small heel again tonight (well, I didn't think I'd be anywhere near Gareth, did I?) and I'm glad I wore them. With a sharp dig downward, my heel thuds on to a foot, and the hand miraculously lets go. I hear the guy swearing (though not the crunch of any bones) but don't look back. Sometimes actions speak louder than words, specially with guys who are too drunk and obnoxious to listen to what you have to say anyway, however polite you might try to be.

God, it's mobbed in here tonight.

Word about the club must be getting out because it's the busiest I've ever seen it. And you know something? Scanning round, there's not a face I recognize. Apart, of course, from Gareth's, up there on the stage, where I'm headed now…

"Hi," a face in the crowd suddenly says to me.

It's one of Anya's sarky boy buddies. I think he must have said "hi" on reflex, before he remembered that I'm a deeply unimportant person.

I hesitate, then lift my arm in a vague gesture of hello. After all, I'm about as keen to talk to Ben as I am to hang around and have a conversation with the drunken yob back there.

"Did you get hold of him, then?"

Oh, it's not Ben; it's the other one, Neil. Ha – I can't tell them *or* their moody faces apart. And now I get it: Neil means did I speak to Gareth after he gave me his number at Anya's on Sunday. What does he want to know for? So him and Ben can have a snigger at my expense again?

I wish I had the sort of brain that could instantaneously come up with snidey put-downs, but sadly, God must have run out of those when I was born. Instead, I ended up with one that stalls when I get worried, so instead of saying what I really want to say (i.e. "What business is it of yours?"), all I can manage is a mumbled "Scuse me" as I leave Neil behind and carry on towards the stage.

Still, he's lucky he didn't get to sample my old heel-in-the-foot trick…

"Hi, Jude!"

Funny, isn't it? One broad smile and an enthusiastic hello from Gareth and all the knots of dread in my stomach melt clean away. I can almost *feel* the anger and worry slither away from my soul. No one who's been *deliberately* ignoring you could smile a smile as warm and wonderful as that, could they?

"Hi!" I grin, stepping up the couple of stairs and joining Gareth on the stage.

"I didn't think I'd see you here tonight!" he says, slipping his headphones off his ears and laying them around his neck. "Didn't you tell me at Anya's that your mate's birthday party was happening tonight?"

And didn't you tell me at Anya's that you would absolutely, definitely phone me on Saturday? I think, but don't say, not now that I can see there's not a glimpse of malice in his face. Instead, I just answer Gareth's question.

"Yeah, my friend Dean's 18th. I was there, but it turned out more of a family thing."

You're telling *me* it was a family thing. Dean's family, Adam's family (half of whom are Dean's family too), Shaunna's family (in-laws of Adam's family) and Molly's family (future in-laws of Dean's family, the way things are going between those two). And little odd-one-out me.

"Hold on two seconds!" says Gareth, spotting what I can't see – someone right behind me by the stage, desperate for a request.

Gareth puts his hand on the small of my back as he leans forward to hear what the guy is asking for, and it feels comfortable and possessive, like he's happy to let the world know I'm with him.

And at the moment, the world includes a familiar group of girls' faces in the sea of dancers; five sets of eyes giving me the evil eye. I don't know their names, apart from Lisa, and Donna, of course. Um, what was it Gareth said before about Lisa getting it all wrong? That Donna *didn't* want to get back with him? I might have to disagree with him on that one if Donna's poisonous expression is anything to go by…

"No problem, mate!" Gareth says to the departing guy, and straightens up beside me. I'm trying to work out how to bring up the subject of Donna and her bad vibes without pointing into the crowd, when Gareth talks first.

"Listen, I'm sorry I didn't get back to you this week, Jude. Everything went a bit mad – college laid tonnes of course work on us and then a DJ friend of mine got flu and I ended up having to stand in for him at all his gigs."

"That's OK." I shrug, happy to have a pretty straightforward explanation after making up so many mad ones in my head all week. (He'd been knocked down by a bus and was in a coma/he was mugged on the way home from the party and had his phone (and my number) stolen/he'd decided that kissing me was the most tragic mistake he'd ever made in his life and he never wanted to see me again/kissing me had repulsed him so much he decided to go back out with Donna…)

"Oh, hey, you couldn't do me a favour, could you, Jude?"

Kiss you again? No problem…

"What?" I ask him.

"Can you get me a bottle of water? It's boiling in here tonight and I'm dying of thirst…"

"Don't be silly!" I laugh, feeling slightly offended when he holds out some money to pay for it. "I'll get it!"

"Thanks, Jude," he smiles gratefully, giving my waist a squeeze before I head for the bar.

I'm grinning like an idiot, I can feel it. The people I'm slipping past on the dancefloor on the way to the bar probably think I'm on drugs or something, the way I'm beaming. But why shouldn't I? I don't think I'm jumping the gun here but I think tonight is the night when I might officially cross over from being Gareth's friend to being Gareth's *girl*friend. (Fingers very tightly crossed.) Shaunna and Molly are probably *well* mad at me right now, but wait till I tell them tomorrow. They'll be so—

Goodbye, brilliant mood.

So long, feel-good feeling.

Another familiar face in the crowd has just sent my sense of excitement into free-fall…

She's got her head tilted back, shrieking so much at whatever joke her friends have just made that she's practically spilling her full pint of beer over her "Babe" T-shirt. And even from where I'm standing, I can see she's a) not wearing a bra, and b) wearing way too much shiny highlighter on her cheeks. What does she think she looks like? And more importantly…

"What are you doing here?" I ask her.

Her usual crew of university mates – including Toy-Boy Will – seem to take a few steps back from us.

"Hey, Jude!" Helen grins infuriatingly in response. "I didn't know you came here!"

You never know where I go because you never ask, I fume silently to myself.

"I come here all the time!"

And I feel like adding, "It's *my* place!" But then I don't want to sound like I'm a five year old in a huffle-puffle 'cause someone's nicked a turn with my tricycle.

"Do you?" Helen widens her eyes, and I see she's wearing mascara and eyeshadow too. "It's great, isn't it? Pete and Alastair heard about it and said we should give it a try tonight."

She gazes around the mobbed club, her head nodding in time to The Avalanches track that Gareth's just put on. I know this is insane but I really feel like *slapping* her all of a sudden.

"So are you here with Shaunna and Molly, then?" she asks, dragging her attention back to me. (Gee, thanks.)

Then I notice it – I notice the stupid, idiotic glint of the tiny diamanté stud in her nose.

"What the hell's that?" I explode.

"Calm down! It's just a piercing, same as yours, Jude! I got it done today. Don't you like it?"

Can you believe her?

"You just don't get it, do you?" I hear myself shout at her. "You're thirty-seven years old. You're my *mother*. Stop acting like you're *my* age and copying what I do! I'm seventeen, I *belong* here. *You* look ridiculous!"

Out of the corner of my eye I see a certain red-head skulking by. But she's the least of my worries right now.

"Jude!" Helen frowns at me. "What's your problem?"

What's my problem? What *is* my problem? I can't even sort out in my brain what exactly my main problem is since I've been worrying myself stupid over plenty of problems lately. And then it's like I've had a blister that's been nagging me but finally goes *splat*...

"I've spoken to Dad," I hear myself announce bluntly. "I've seen him, I mean. And my little brother."

From a distance, I could add, but I don't.

"*What?*"

Helen's face is frozen in surprise; but I can practically hear the scream that must be going on inside her head.

"Oliver. That's his name. His mother – Maggie – she looks quite pretty. Dad showed me her photo."

Now, it's like I really *have* smacked Helen in the face.

"Helen? Are you OK?" asks Toy-Boy, spotting that something's up and coming to interfere.

I feel myself start to shake and walk away fast; there's nothing else I want to say to her and nothing I want to hear back.

With wavery hands, I try and scoop my money out of my bag, determined to get on with my life as normal, as if *she* wasn't here. And that starts with getting Gareth the drink I promised him from the bar.

Only I don't quite end up there...

"You waiting to go in?" a girl and a boy in matching long, black coats ask me.

I idly wonder what type of make-up goths use. It's sleeting hard tonight, but their white faces, burgundy-tinged lipstick and black eye make-up are run-free and pristine. Unlike my make-up, which is probably halfway down my face. (That's what crying and standing in torrential sleet does for you.)

"No, I'm not waiting," I tell them, my teeth chattering.

They eye me up and down – some mad girl hovering outside a club dressed only in a pair of boots, black trousers and an off-the-shoulder top – and shuffle inside.

God. How did this happen? That's what I've been trying to figure out for the last five minutes, in between blubbing in a sorry-for-myself way and catching double pneumonia. And then I get that lightbulb-above-the-head moment: it was that girl, Lisa. She was passing when I was talking to (make that *yelling* at) Helen. She must have heard me say I was seventeen and ratted on me to one of the staff. After all, that guy who stopped me before I got to the bar and asked me for proof of age – how *else* would he have known that I was under-18?

Oh, the *shame*, the deep, deep *shame* of being asked to leave, without being allowed to tell Gareth what was happening, or even to go and fetch my coat, all while my stupid mother and that bitch of a girl Lisa carry on enjoying themselves regardless...

As the door swings closed behind the goth couple, it's kicked back open again and the burly, unsmiling bar manager strides out, holding a bundle of brown suede and fur at arm's-length like it's road kill or something.

"This it?"

"Yeah..." I say flatly, taking my coat from him.

"Took a while to find. It wasn't on the seat you said it was on – it was on the floor under the table next to it."

Oh. No wonder he was holding it at arm's-length; my pride and joy Afghan is now lightly soaked in spilled beer and smells like an ashtray. Still, *it's* warm, and *I'm* not, so there's nothing to do but slip it on and hope no one tries to offer me their spare change as I walk through the city centre or tells me the way to the nearest rough sleeper hostel.

The slam of the club door as the bar manager abandons me to the elements leaves me alone with only sleet for company. There's nothing I can do but turn my collar up (feeling – urgh! – a trickle of ash slither down my neck) and head for home.

In front of me, car headlights twinkle through the rain, and above there's not a glimmer of a star to guide me on my miserable way. I wonder, is there anyone else out there in the universe feeling *quite* as humiliated and depressed as I do right now?

The only thing that's going to see me through the next few hours is cigarettes, Pringles and sad, sad music played very, VERY loud. And if old Mr Watson next door doesn't like that, he can stuff it up his tartan dressing gown…

chapter fourteen

 *Small pleasures*

Date: *Friday 13th December*

Stressometer rating: *Low. Thanks to a little help from my friends.*

Wish of the moment: *More fun in my life, please.*

What's bad in my life: stuff to do with Dad, Gareth and Helen. What's good in my life: friends, small pleasures and streamers. (Don't worry, I'll explain.)

If you want a resumé of the bad stuff, it runs like this: no, my dad still hasn't phoned me to arrange getting together again. (Can't he find a measly two minutes in the space of two weeks to call me?) *No*, Gareth hasn't replied to the message I left explaining what went on at the club. I mean, even if he had *more* course work, even if he was *still* covering for his sick DJ mate, he could have picked up the phone at *some* point to commiserate with me about what happened. Unless, of course, he's decided that it's too uncool to hang out with an under-age girl. Nah … come on. This is kind, considerate Gareth we're talking about – not one of Anya's poseur pals. And *no*, my mother and I aren't exactly talking to each other.

Here's an edited version (i.e. minus the swear words) of our conversation last Saturday.

HELEN: Oh, Jude – I'm glad I caught you before you went to work. Your bedroom light was off when I got in last night and I didn't want to wake you.
ME: I haven't got time for this, Helen.
HELEN: Oh, come on, Jude! You can't just say what you said last night and then disappear, and expect me not to want to ask you about it!
ME (*gritting my teeth*): I didn't just "disappear" – something came up. Look, I've got to go – I'll be late.
HELEN: Listen, you can spare me two minutes. Please tell me what you meant about seeing your father…
ME: Hey, how about this: *I'll* tell you about Dad, if *you* admit that it's a really crap idea for a mother to turn up at the same club as her daughter!
HELEN: Why? Why should that be a problem?
ME: Because … because it's a total embarrassment, Helen!
HELEN: So, you're saying I'm not allowed to have fun? At my age I should be going to bingo or sitting at home with my slippers or doing crossword puzzles?!
ME: If you're just going to make jokes and not even *try* to understand me, then I don't see what we have to talk about!

Exit me, and cue a huffy silence in our house for the whole

of the last week. Anyway, enough of the gloomy stuff; let's talk about streamers.

It's amazing what you can do with streamers. You can transform a dull school hall into a slightly more cheery school hall. You can have hours of fun running around and chucking them over each other (instead of pinning them up around the hall, which was the reason you got excused from classes this afternoon in the first place). You can even write swear words with them.

You want proof?

"Gerroff!" I pant breathlessly, after scrambling on top of a table to get away from Shaunna and Molly.

Course, it's a bit late now to tell my friends to leave me alone, considering the fact that they've been chasing me for the last five minutes and have tangled me up in so many metres of coloured streamers that I could pass for a Christmas tree, no problem.

Shaunna and Molly are panting too, exhausted from ganging up on me and laughing too much.

"Do you give in, Jude?" Shaunna grins up at me.

"Definitely," I reply, enjoying acting like a care free five-year-old kid for once instead of a seventeen year old with all the worries of the world on my shoulders. "So whose turn is it next? Molly?"

"Don't you dare!" splutters Molly, backing away from me and Shaunna.

But Shaunna's attention is momentarily distracted.

"Oh, good grief – check out what Kyle Jacobs has done!"

Me and Molly look where Shaunna is pointing. Kyle Jacobs is currently on a stepladder at the other end of the hall from us, putting the final touches to his streamer work of art. It's our year's Christmas party tonight and everyone else here this afternoon – everyone helping decorate the hall – has chosen traditional draping loops around the cavernous room. But not Kyle, oh no. He's opted to spell out something *particularly* rude in very big letters.

"Oi, Kyle!" Shaunna yells over. "Are you going to leave it like that?"

Kyle, now clambering down the ladder and standing back to admire his handiwork better, turns and grins in our direction.

"Definitely!" he yells back, as several other people stop what they're doing to gawp and giggle at his masterpiece. "You can only read it from certain angles, so let's see how quick it takes the teachers to spot it!"

Kyle once got reported to the headmaster after telling our careers adviser that he wanted to be an anti-globalization protester when he left school. I don't know what qualifications you need for that but I guess getting expelled from school might be good for his urban guerrilla CV.

"Kyle should get a photo of that tonight: you know, with some of the teachers dancing obliviously underneath it," I say, lowering myself down off the table to join Shaunna and Molly now that our game of catch-chase seems to be safely over. "The Tate Modern would definitely pay to have that on their walls!"

Hey, look: I've made a kind of joke. In fact, I've spent the last 90 minutes doing nothing but fooling around and having a laugh. Who'd have guessed? Exactly one week ago, I was so gloomy that I couldn't ever imagine grinning again. But thanks to super-human efforts by my two brilliant friends, I'm doing my best to enjoy the small pleasures.

"It's like this, Jude," Molly had told me last Saturday night, when we were round at her place for a post-mortem of my traumatic Friday evening. "You've got no control over the big stuff going on in your life, so you might as well enjoy the small stuff."

"Small pleasures are what get you through times of big poo," Shaunna agreed, putting it more succinctly.

I didn't really see that at first – even though the Pringles and loud sad music on Friday night *had* kind of helped take the edge off my misery – but Shaunna and Mol kept drumming it into me by doing sweet stuff like treating me to a day out on Sunday. (Feeding the ducks in the park, comfort food, going skating, comfort food, seeing a funny movie, *more* comfort food.) By the time I was eating my second knickerbocker glory of the day, I began to see their point. I might have spent hours moaning and dissecting my problems with them, but reluctantly I had to admit that I'd still managed to have a pretty good time, despite myself.

So although my pride is still in tatters and my heart still feels like it's been run over by a juggernaut, I'm doing my best to keep happy, with a little help from my friends. Despite all the stress, there is – as Shaunna and Molly keep reminding me – lots of good stuff going on in my life (even some stuff which *doesn't* involve comfort food). There's Mol and Shaunna not holding it against me that I did a runner from Dean's birthday party on Friday, for a start. Then there's Dean and Adam being really sweet and saying they'll boycott the club after me getting chucked out so unceremoniously. God, I'm even looking forward to this dumb old school Christmas party tonight, just because it's bound to be silly, straightforward, un-trendy fun…

"Hey, I've changed my mind about wearing that purple top tonight," says Shaunna, untangling swathes of streamers from her hands. "It's too clingy. It makes me feel like Pamela Anderson."

Me and Molly catch each other's eyes and start snickering. Like us, Shaunna isn't exactly over-endowed in the bosom department. She was even joking last week that she'd need to wear two Wonderbras at the same time – stuffed with an entire roll of loo paper – to fool anyone into thinking she had a cleavage.

"Well, it doesn't make me feel like Pamela Anderson, *exactly*," she corrects herself. "But it's still too tight. I tried it on again last night and it's cutting off the circulation under my arms. So … anyone fancy a bit of a shopping trip after school today?"

"Yeah, why not?" I say, as me and Molly both shrug and nod in agreement.

Hey, maybe I should spoil myself and get a new stud or ring for my eyebrow, now that it's finally healed properly. A jewelled one, I think: that would go well with the necklace I'm going to be wearing for the party. Another small pleasure…

"Great. I've seen some nice stuff in Miss Selfridge. We could try there first and then—"

And then a tuneless trill from my nearby bag interrupts what Shaunna is saying. It's my mobile, but it's not playing "Hey Jude", which means I'm not about to hear the long-lost voices of either my father or Gareth any second now.

"A text?" asks Molly, as I dig my phone out of the

bottom of my cluttered bag.

"Yep," I nod, checking out the screen.

"Who's it from?"

"Wait a minute," I tell Shaunna, as I read what's written. "I don't know yet..."

"Well, what's it say, then?" Shaunna demands, not giving in that easily.

"It says, *'Meet me 2-night, 8.30, outside shopping mall. Can't call – phone playing up. Luv –'*"

"Love who?" Molly says excitedly.

"Hold on... I have to scroll down," I tell her, cursing how small the buttons on my mobile are for my normal-sized (but shaky) fingers. "*'Luv, Gareth'*. And there's a kiss!"

"*Ooh-OOO-oooh!*" Molly and Shaunna tease me in unison.

"God, he got back to me! He wants to see me!"

Out of the three things in my life that are resolutely rubbish at the moment, here's one that's suddenly got a *whole* lot better. My entire chest is instantly racked with a pain that I think is pure happiness...

"That's great!" squeals Molly, hugging me.

"Yeah, but he wants to meet you at 8.30 p.m... What about the party?" frowns Shaunna.

"She could phone him, though. You could phone him, Jude, and just get him to change the time! You could meet him at teatime instead, or on your lunch-break from work tomorrow or something."

I appreciate what Molly's saying, and I am a little torn about the idea of missing out on the party, but really, that doesn't matter so much now I know that Gareth wants to see me. Anyway, I couldn't change the time even if I wanted to.

"But I can't call – he says his phone's bust, remember?" I tell my friends, holding my mobile out so they can examine his message for themselves.

They scan it, and look crestfallen.

"But how could he text if his phone's broken?" Shaunna suddenly points out.

"*I* don't know," I reply, slightly irritated by my best friend getting picky over details. "It must be just a glitch. The text function's working but the talking part isn't. Whatever... I'm not a phone engineer."

"Aw, Jude," sighs Molly, oblivious to the techno hassles. "I'm really chuffed for you and everything, but it won't be the same without you tonight!"

"What about when the teachers stand under Kyle's swear words?" Shaunna chips in. "You're going to miss all that!"

"I know, but..."

But I don't have to explain any more to my friends; they understand all right.

"We can still go shopping and get ready together. Me and Mol will get you looking *so* good for your date!"

"Well, I wouldn't exactly call it a *date*, Shaunnie," I laugh self-consciously.

But I'm hoping against hope that that's *exactly* what it is...

chapter fifteen

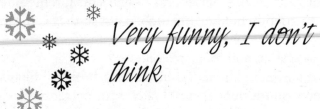

Very funny, I don't think

Date:	❄	*Friday 13th December*
Stressometer rating:	❄	*High. Is tonight the night?*
Wish of the moment:	❄	*That I'd listened to my gran...*

Have you ever seen those corny, free catalogues you some-times get inside newspapers? Those ones that sell hundreds of entirely useless gadgets like roll-up jigsaw puzzle mats, complex spider catchers and special grips for people who aren't strong enough to open their crisp packets without help?

You get the idea. Well, usually I skim through those just for the pleasure of seeing what amazingly naff inventions have been added to the catalogue. (Gloves that change colour with your body heat? I'll take two pairs, please!) Anyway, one thing that's always advertised in there is the giant slipper – a big, fleecy boot thing that you're meant to slip both your feet in. I always used to wonder how you were meant to get up to go to the loo or make a cup of tea or whatever when you were wearing it, but suddenly I have this moment of clarity: the giant slipper is *the* most fantastic invention ever and I'd give *anything* to slip my icy-cold feet into one right this second. And my gran; doesn't she always witter on about thermals? Now I understand that she isn't a deranged old lady with no sense of style; she's a woman with incredible common sense. And that thermal vest she gave me as a birthday present? I really wish I hadn't donated it to the local charity shop when I was having that last big clear-out in my room…

Boy, it's bitterly cold sitting here on this bench. *And* pretty boring, to tell the truth. In fact, I'm frozen, bored and *anxious* all at the same time. This is giving me an ulcer, never mind frostbite.

What a difference a few hours makes. When me and my friends were here earlier – finding Shaunna the perfect black gypsy top – the mall was buzzing with shoppers and noise and bustle. Now the mall entrance is shuttered and dark, and the only noise is the swoosh of cars careering through the giant puddles of water that are clogging the high street's gutters after the recent downpour.

Another source of noise, of course, was from the bundle of guys that passed me by a couple of minutes ago, roaring and yelling at each other like a bunch of baying, feuding bears. I don't suppose they were the same lads who hassled me when I first turned up at the club last week, but they're part of that same tradition of loud and boozy boys. Before they'd stumbled into view, I'd been trying to distract myself by imagining what was going on back in the school hall; wondering whether Kyle Jacobs and his secret swear words had been rumbled yet and whether or not Shaunna and Molly were managing to have a good time without me. But as soon as I saw (and heard the roar) of the booze-hounds, my mind immediately made that connection between them and the club, and that was it: I was back to fretting.

The fact is, "Loaded" should be starting up about now, which means Gareth will be there, and not here with me, which makes no sense at all. And it doesn't make any sense that I've been waiting here for him in the cold and damp for an hour now, and he hasn't tried to phone or text me to let me know what's going on.

What *is* going on? He's always been so sweet and caring whenever we've talked; so sympathetic about all the stuff with Dad. How can he treat me this way? Was I just fooling myself, by thinking that tonight was the night we were going to get together for sure?

This is pathetic, I know, but in-between getting Gareth's text message and turning up here, I got it into my head that he was going to tell me he was so mad about me getting booted out of the club last week that he'd chucked in his job there. I'd daydreamed that we end up in some cosy little caff tonight, huddled over mugs of hot chocolate, watching people hurrying by outside in the wintry street while we sat in the warmth, holding hands and talking about how all that mattered was being together. Or maybe he'd take me back to his flat and I'd see all the amazing paintings he'd told me he'd done at art school. Maybe he'd end up asking me to pose for him. Well, every famous artist has their muse, don't they?

Jude, you *idiot*. Welcome to the real (wet) world...

That's it – bang goes my mascara again, and the lovely eye make-up that Molly did specially for me. God, I've been going through so many paper hankies in the last few weeks that Kleenex will be sending me a gold-plated man-size box of tissues as a gift to honour their most prized customer. Their profits must be going through the roof, thanks to me and my rotten life. *Nothing* goes right for me; think about it – Helen's nose piercing wasn't even the *tiniest* bit red and swollen on the first day she got it done, while my eyebrow is already itching and throbbing angrily thanks to the pretty new stud I splashed out on this afternoon. See what I mean about nothing going right for me?

(I'm sorry, Shaunna and Molly – I'm just too blue right now to see the small pleasures anywhere...)

More footsteps, more voices, more happy people on the way to somewhere great tonight, with fun in mind. Without looking up, I can tell by the tone of the voices and the giggles that it's girls this time, not lairy lads.

I'm just about to sink back into my pit of gloom when more giggles – high-pitched cackles, even – disturb my moping. I glance up and see – *instantly* see – what this has *all* been about...

I barge through the swing doors, straight past Mr Davidson the Physics teacher, and Mr Whaled the Maths teacher, who must be acting as school bouncers tonight.

"Bit late, aren't we, Jude? There's only ten minutes to go!" Mr Whaled calls after me, as I hurry down the corridor towards the sound of music booming from the hall.

"What happened – couldn't decide what to wear? What

are you girls like!" I hear Mr Davidson joke. Well, Mr Whaled seems to think it's funny, since they both burst out laughing.

Can't say I'm in the mood for laughing much – all I want to do is find my two best friends, and tell them just what's happened to me, before I go *totally* mad.

Celine Jones and Susie McKenzie are just coming out of the hall as I'm about to go in.

"Seen Shaunna or Molly?" I ask them, hoping they're not going to say that the party's so naff that my friends scarpered hours ago (always a possibility, but not one I wanted to hear about right now).

"I saw them dancing a while ago, over by Kyle Jacobs's sign. The one that says—"

"I know what it says, Celine," I break in. "How long ago was that?"

"I dunno. 'Bout quarter of an hour, maybe. Wasn't it, Susie?"

"I guess. Hey, are you all right, Jude? You look a bit…"

It's nice of Susie to be concerned, but I don't hang around to listen to the rest of what she's got to say. Instead, I speed into the packed, darkened room, full of smiling, dancing, laughing people, and immediately feel like a small black cloud slipping into a sunny, blue sky. Not that they seem to notice me as I push my way through; they're all having too good a time, singing along and waving their hands in the air to that old Christmas duet that Robbie Williams did with Nicole Kidman.

"Somethin' Stupid" – that's what it's called. Kind of sums me up right now, when you think about it…

And then I spot one arm in particular waving along in

time; an arm with a black lace-edged sleeve fluttering at the elbow. And right behind Shaunna and her floaty gypsy top, I catch a glimpse of Molly's bright, white blonde hair, like a beacon guiding me over.

"Jude!" Shaunna squeals in delight when she sees me.

Half a second later, her face falls when she clocks my expression.

"That bad?" Molly asks, rushing to put an arm around me.

"Worse…" I say, before I start blubbing properly in the warmth of their kindness.

"The only good thing," says Shaunna, taking the milk out of the microwave and pouring it into the brightly coloured mugs in front of us, "is that it still means things could be OK between you and Gareth. If he had nothing to do with any of this, I mean."

It's late; the three of us are back at Shaunna's place, all still dressed in party mode and huddled round her breakfast bar.

"What? It could *still* be OK, even though he hasn't bothered getting in touch?" I manage a wry smile, as I watch Molly take over and stir our hot chocolates. "Nice try, Shaunnie, but I think it's fair to say that me and Gareth aren't set to be the next Posh and Becks."

Shaunna gives a little shrug, unaware that she's now trailing her lacy black sleeve through a puddle of splashed milk on the work-top.

"And anyway," I continue, "I don't know how right it *could* be, if he's got a horrible ex-girlfriend hanging around who likes to play vicious games…"

Shaunna can't argue with that. Both my friends agree that it looks like I was right royally set up tonight. It wasn't Gareth who'd texted me – it was Donna, or one of her cronies, who'd done it. I knew that for sure when I glanced up from the bench outside the shopping mall earlier and saw Donna and Lisa and the others on the opposite side of the road, dressed up for the club, sheltering under umbrellas, and pausing to laugh their heads off at the sight of their practical joke going so well.

What a prize mug I must have looked, slumped there waiting in vain on that dingy, damp bench…

"How would they have got your number?" asks Molly.

"Gareth still hangs about with Donna, as a 'friend', remember," I sigh. "Maybe she was noseying at his phone's address list."

"But didn't his number show up when you got that message?"

I shrug at Shaunna's question. "I can't remember. I was too chuffed just to see his name at the end of the text."

"The thing is," Molly points out, "if Donna was sly enough to look up your number in his address list, then she's sly enough to text you from his phone, if he left it lying around."

"Who knows…" I sigh. "All I *do* know is she's behind this."

"Here's to Donna and her coven of witches," Shaunna announces, lifting her mug high in a toast. "Here's hoping they all catch an unpleasant disease soon. I hear scarlet fever's pretty nasty…"

"Hear, hear," me and Molly join in, clunking our mugs together.

Good old Shaunna; she can't make this situation any less awful for me, but at least she knows the right things to say.

And so does her mum.

"Jude; something for you, dear," says Mrs Sullivan, padding into the kitchen in her slippers and handing me a tube of Savlon. "I noticed when you came in that, that … er … *thingumee* on your eyebrow was looking a little inflamed. A little dab of this should sort it out for you."

Not for the first time, I fantasize about asking Mrs Sullivan if I can move in. There's a spare room going begging since Shaunna's sister Ruth moved out.

Yep, I've decided – the only way to solve my problems is to become a hermit and live quietly in Shaunna's spare room, where I can spend my days healing my broken heart and trashed pride, drinking hot chocolate and having my brow soothed by Mrs Sullivan, who's very good at that sort of thing.

The only question is, when can I move in…?

chapter sixteen

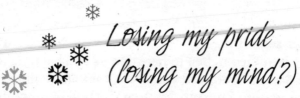

*Losing my pride
(losing my mind?)*

Date: *Friday 20th December*

**Stressometer
rating:**   *High. I'm a desperate girl.*

**Wish of the
moment:**   *That I get a happy ending
(fat chance).*

Some number-crunching exercises for you…

1) It has been exactly 17 days since I saw my father, i.e.
17 days since he promised to get in touch and arrange a
time that we could get together before Christmas. There
are now five days till Christmas. (Why do I get a feeling
this isn't looking good?)

2) The number of times I have called my dad: once.

3) The number of times I have hung up when calling my
dad: once ('cause Maggie answered the phone and I bottled it).

4) It has been exactly 14 days since I saw Gareth, since
the night my pride and I were kicked out of the club.

5) The number of messages I've left on his mobile: four (I would have left more, but I feel four is *just* the right side of desperate – and anyway, Shaunna and Molly have banned me from phoning him again).

6) The number of times Gareth has got back to me: none.

So, why have I been phoning Gareth, when just one week ago I was on the verge of admitting to myself that nothing was *ever* going to go on between us? Because of a stupid late night movie I saw, *that's* why. Pathetic, I know, and it sounds even *more* pathetic when I tell you that it was some lousy American made-for-TV movie, and I missed the start so I didn't even know what it was supposed to be about. All I caught was this cute guy, practically sobbing to his mate about how his girlfriend was accusing him of this, that and whatever. "She's got no trust, Brad," his mate comforted him. "That's the problem. She *owes* you that, man. And if there's no trust, then there's nothing…" Normally, dialogue (and acting) that's *that* bad would send me reaching for the bin to barf in, but maybe all my senses are on hyper-alert or something at the moment, 'cause next thing I knew I was blubbing like a baby and listening to my heart telling me I've got to trust Gareth and give him another chance.

Well, right now, I'm giving him the biggest chance he'll ever get, and quite possibly giving myself a double dose of the flu at the same time. (Will Gareth appreciate that I'm losing my mind, my dignity and quite possibly my health for his sake?)

I pull the scarf around my neck up a little higher and try to distract myself from the cold and my nerves by concentrating on my conversation with Shaunna.

"I think I'd quite *like* to have a semi-naked, fit, twentysomething guy wandering around my house first thing in the morning," says Shaunna, offering me a mint. "It would sure brighten the place up. All I get a glimpse of is a middle-aged man in stripy pyjamas making horrible gargling noises in the bathroom."

"But that's the point, isn't it?" I answer her through a mouthful of chewy mint. "I'd rather walk into the bathroom and find *my* dad making horrible gargling noises than find my mother's pre-pubescent lover standing there in his boxers squeezing his spots in the mirror or whatever he was doing today."

Another quick number-crunch… Nights that Helen has let Will the Toy-Boy stay over in the last three weeks: five. It started out just being Saturday night, but judging by this morning, she's upped it to weeknight visitations too. God, is it only going to be a matter of time before he starts leaving his toothbrush and smelly socks at our place? Helen pays me little enough attention as it is – with Will the Toy-Boy around, I'll just turn totally invisible in my own home…

"Well, I still think I'd rather have your mother than mine. At least Helen doesn't mind what you get up to. Do you know what my mum did yesterday?"

I shake my head at Shaunna, while considering something she just said… "Helen doesn't mind what you get up to." I think I'd phrase it more like this: "Helen doesn't give a damn what you get up to." And another problem with that point is that I don't get up to anything, i.e. I haven't got a *life*.

"I was fifteen minutes late – fifteen minutes! – getting

back from Adam's," Shaunna blathers on, stomping her feet to keep the frostbite from her toes, "and my over-excitable mother only goes and phones my sister in a panic, telling her she's sure something's happened to me and should she phone the police and the hospital? I tell you what she should do – she should *stop treating me like a baby*! I mean, if she knew I was standing here in the freezing cold, that'd be it – she'd convince herself I was going to come down with bronchitis or TB or something…"

"Well, you didn't *have* to come," I point out slightly testily. I know that Shaunna thinks that hovering outside the back entrance of the "Loaded" club in the hope of catching Gareth go in is both sad and dumb ("Are you *insane*? Do you realize how *desperate* that's going to look?" she'd said at first.) But it was something I had to do. And as she was the one who was so determined to come with me to show me a bit of support ("I might think it's insane, but I'm not going to let you go there on your own, Jude!"), I'd rather she didn't moan on about it, even in a back-handed way.

"Don't get grouchy with me just 'cause you're uptight!" Shaunna frowns at me. "Maybe I don't think this is such an excellent idea—"

"Yes, I *know*. You think I'm chasing him," I interrupt her. "But what about you and Adam? Don't you regret that it took you a whole year to give *him* a chance?"

Oh, yeah. Shaunna can't exactly lecture me about love when she spent 12 months doing stuff like pining after a guy who was a total stranger *and* dating Dean, all the while treating adorable Adam like he was about as appealing as a wisdom tooth pushing through.

"*Course* I regret that," she mumbles. "OK, fair point. But I still don't see why you've got to give him a second chance by hovering in a grotty back alley…"

I could point out it's because it's the only place I know I can catch him for sure but I've said all that already, so instead I just smile at her, glad of her company. It's not as if Donna and her cronies would use this staff entrance to the club, but the thought of that lot somehow catching sight of me loitering around again like Jude No-Mates made me feel slightly ill.

Actually, I nearly had Molly here tonight too – she was all set to blow out Dean, even though he'd already bought tickets in advance for the new Tom Cruise movie. But I told her I'd be OK with just Shaunna. 'Cause let's face it, two's company, but three might look like a lynch mob to Gareth…

"And I guess Gareth's a nice guy, like you say, Jude," says Shaunna, linking her arm in mine, "so it's maybe worth talking to him, to see if you can figure out what's been going on."

Aw … that's really sweet of her to say, specially since I know she doesn't mean a word of it. It's just that her and Molly have already mumbled about being deeply unimpressed by Gareth's lack of contact, no matter what his track record is. ("Don't care how sweet he's been to you, Jude – if he can't pick up a phone then he's verging on jerkdom," was how Shaunna subtly put it the other night.)

But the way I see it is, we really had the start of something going, me and Gareth. And now … well, *something* must have happened to make him cool off. Could that be down to his less-than-lovely, not-quite-ex, Donna? I mean, if she was behind last Friday's prank text message (and I'm 99.9% sure she was), then maybe she's managed to poison Gareth against me. Who knows? But I need to find out, even if the truth hurts. And here comes my chance. Oh, God, I feel so sick with nerves that I'll probably puke on his Vans and he'll never want to see me again anyway…

It takes him a second to spot us after he slams the taxi door shut – it's pretty poorly lit round here in the alley, away from the street lights and beams from streams of passing traffic.

"Hey! How're you doing, Jude?" Gareth smiles warmly at me, and gives Shaunna a friendly nod hello. He's weighted down with a big box of records, and has another bag of them trailing off his shoulder. Maybe struggling with that lot is what stops him from coming and giving me a kiss hello. (Wishful thinking.)

Help … I'm suddenly so confused. What body signals is he sending out? That smile looks too genuine, so Donna can't have turned him against me. But what's with the lack of physical contact? Why is he standing so far away? It's like we've time-travelled back to *way* beyond the kiss at Anya's flat.

"Hi, Gareth," I croak. "Did you… Did you get my message?"

"Yeah, sure…" he nods, as aware as I am that it was messages *plural*. "Meant to get back to you, Jude, but everything's been mad, with the end of term and loads of parties and stuff to DJ for."

"Oh, right. Yeah, of course," I hear myself babbling. "Well, it's just that … well, me and Shaunna were passing, and I thought I'd look out for you, that's all."

What a pathetic lie! Just passing? Why the hell would we be "just passing" the alleyway at the back of the club? Damn – I really should have worked out what I was going to say a little better. But that would take brains, and I don't really have any that aren't scrambled right now.

"Right…" Gareth nods, hauling his heavy record box up in his arms. "By the way, that was really bad luck getting booted out by Benny the bar manager. Specially since half the people in the club are under-age anyway!"

"Tell me about it," I try to say lightly. "Um … that's what I wanted to mention tonight. If I saw you, I mean. Just to explain that I didn't run out on you that night, after I went to get your drink. It's just … well, I know I told you that on the messages I left on your phone and everything, but I thought I'd tell you myself, in case you didn't get those messages. For some reason. It's just, y'know, your mobile could have been broken or something."

I sense Shaunna shuffle uncomfortably beside me, like some micro-signal to tell me to shut up and stop waffling so moronically. But it's no use, my mouth has got verbal diarrhoea and I can't stop myself.

"But then your phone *must* be working, since you *did* get my messages. Ha, ha! Anyway, there was something else I wanted to tell you. Or ask you about. About this text message I got last Friday. From you. Only it wasn't from you, was it?"

Gareth looks truly confused, and who could blame him since I'm probably coming across like an escapee from the psycho bunny-boiler hospital.

"Jude got this text last Friday afternoon, supposedly from you," Shaunna butts in to help me out. "It was asking her to meet you at half-eight by the entrance to the shopping mall."

The fact that she's speaking English and not gibberish (like me) makes it a whole lot easier for Gareth to understand what's going on.

"From me?" he frowns, glancing back and forth between me and Shaunna. "God, no – that wasn't from me. I wouldn't have said that time anyway; I'd have been on my way here by then…"

"Yeah, we reckoned that. But someone's played a trick on Jude, and we're just trying to work out who," Shaunna continues.

Frowning some more, Gareth shakes his head, obviously flummoxed.

"I thought… I thought it might have something to do with Donna," I hear myself suggest accusingly, finding my voice and then instantly wishing I hadn't, from the shocked look on Gareth's face.

"Donna? Jeez, no – you've got it wrong, Jude! She's a real softie, she wouldn't have it in her to do something like that!"

Huh – Gareth hasn't ever seen the dirty looks I've got off her or heard her laugh herself stupid at me sitting on that bench like a muppet last week. But how do I explain that to him without sounding like I'm slagging off his "friend" Donna too much, specially since he seems to be on the defensive when it comes to her?

"Well, *someone* did it. And it has to be someone from the club who knows both of you," Shaunna points out, folding her arms across her chest, as if she's baiting Gareth to come up with a better suggestion.

"Well, maybe it's Lisa fooling around again…" he mutters. "Like I said before, she's got some crazy idea about me and Donna getting back together."

And she's not the only one, I think to myself, remembering Donna's cackle just as clearly as any of her other bitchy mates.

"Listen, Jude," says Gareth, walking towards me and struggling slightly with his slipping bag and box, "I have to go in and set up now, but I'll try and find out what's gone on, all right?"

"All right…" I whisper.

"I'll get this sorted. *Trust* me. I'll give you a call later – OK?"

I nod, gazing into his soft, amber eyes with those long, fluffy lashes, then feel a rush of pleasure as he leans towards me.

How ridiculous am I? One dry peck on the cheek from Gareth and I'm melting, mumbling a soppy, girly "Bye…" after him as he strides off and backs his way though the staff entrance door.

"It's bound to be that Donna," says Shaunna, as soon as the door clangs shut and we're on our own in the gloomy alley.

"I know," I nod.

"She probably still fancies him, and you're just one big threat."

"I know."

"Gareth doesn't get that though, 'cause she'll be acting all sweetness and light when she's with him, and then turning into a possessive cow behind his back, using all her cronies to intimidate you and scare you off."

"I know."

"Trouble is, Jude – and don't get annoyed with me for saying this – Gareth might side with her. Maybe he likes you, but you've got to remember that he's known her a lot longer – he might be too much of a nice guy to see what she's up to."

"I know."

And I also know that sure as sleet is sleet and snow is snow – Donna or no Donna – I can't let go of Gareth.

I'm miserable, confused, have an ache from my stomach to my throat and feel burning hot, even while the circling snowflakes are settling on my face.

Those symptoms can only mean one thing: I'm in love for sure and there's nothing I can do about it…

chapter seventeen

'Tis the season to be jolly (ho, ho, ho...)

Date: *Wednesday 25th December*

Stressometer rating: *Low. My feelings have been numbed by boredom and classical music.*

Wish of the moment: *That I could have a remotely merry Christmas. As if...*

It sounded like a riot at Shaunna's place when I phoned just now. Shaunna could hardly talk for laughing – as well as Adam, her sister, brother-in-law and gran were all round, and Adam had apparently started up a game of charades by cancan-ing around the room so energetically that he seriously alarmed her gran, who grumpily announced there was no such film as *Moo Lawn Rouge* when he tried to explain what he'd been getting at.

In fact, there was such a clamour of noise and voices and laughter going on in the background that I knew Shaunna was finding it hard to concentrate on our conversation, and straight away I kind of regretted calling her to wish her

Merry Christmas.

"Don't be silly – come over!" she told me, when I said I'd better go and leave her to it.

But I said no. I think I'd feel a bit too much like a saddo, gatecrashing the tail-end of someone else's Christmas Day. Instead, I'll just tune out to some rubbish TV and gaze adoringly at the twenty-centimetre high plastic tree that Helen has stuck on the mantelpiece as our one concession to Christmas decorations.

As I put down the phone, I hear a blast of some carol coming from the telly, which segues immediately into a totally different Christmas-themed pop song, which changes again into the soundtrack of some blockbuster film, which merges at the flick of a button on the remote control into some hysterical canned laughter track.

"Usual Christmas Day crap!" I hear Helen mutter to herself, as the TV goes suddenly silent. Any minute now she'll probably stick on one of her favourite Joni Mitchell albums and start howling along to it while she fixes herself a big glass of wine. What fun – for her, not *me*…

God, it's only 8 p.m. I've been in the house all of four minutes and I've got no idea what to do with myself between now and bedtime. I really hope Helen doesn't want us to *bond* or anything, just 'cause it's the season of kindness and goodwill, blah, blah, blah. It was enough of a struggle to be smiley and polite round at my Aunt Jess's today and I don't have the energy for any more of that.

I mean, picture the scene. My Aunt Jess's new flat is so minimalist that she didn't want to muss up its white airiness with the merest *hint* of a Christmas decoration. Sitting around her undecorated, immaculate bleached wood dining table were: me (smiling, polite, bored out of my brain), Helen (smiling, polite, tanking back a bit too much red wine) and my Aunt Jess (smiling, polite, visibly wincing at the circles of red wine Helen's glass was leaving on her precious bleached wood). In the background, there was a radio tuned to some classical station, and in the foreground, one empty designer dining chair that *should* have contained my gran, only *she* decided at the last minute that it would be much more fun to jet off to Malta for the festive season rather than endure a smiling, polite and uptight Christmas at Aunt Jess's. And who could blame her…?

"Do you want anything?" asks Helen, passing me in the hallway.

I don't know whether she means a drink, some peanuts, a mince pie, a father who keeps his promises or a boyfriend.

"No," I say. I'd say "Yes" in a nanosecond if I thought she meant the last two, but since Helen isn't a witch (well, not the magical sort, anyway), I don't think she can wave a wand and arrange to give me either of *those* as a Christmas present. I think she just meant a drink/peanuts/ mince pies/whatever.

Trust me… That was more-or-less the last thing Gareth said to me when I saw him on Friday night. Well, I'm *still* trying to trust him, but his allergy to the phone is stretching my patience and heartstrings to the verge of snapping…

"Thanks again for the CD, by the way, Jude," Helen says, pausing as she heads into the kitchen. "I'm sure I'll really like it."

I'm not sure if she will, but at least the Erykah Badu album was recorded sometime within living memory, unlike most of the stuff she listens to. You'd think she'd want to be more up-to-date with her musical choices, to impress all her student buddies.

"No problem," I reply, trying once again to avoid looking at the twinkle of gemstone at the side of her nose. (I'm back to wearing my plain silver bar stud in my eyebrow, since the pretty, delicate ring I bought made it seep yellow pus, despite the Savlon Mrs Sullivan made me put on it.)

"D'you want to get that?" Helen calls out, already on the search for wine as the doorbell trings loudly.

"Whatever." I shrug, even though she can't see that.

But what I *can* see is a tall silhouette in the glass doorway. It can only be a man's silhouette, and for one nerve-jangling, mad moment I imagine it's Dad, come to play Santa Claus and happy families, even if it is just for one night only. But then...

"Hi, Jude!" Will the Toy-Boy says breezily, as he walks in without a second's hesitation and hands me a bottle of wine before he begins hauling his coat off. "Is Helen here?"

"You bet! And I'm armed and dangerous, so you better be careful!" my mother giggles coquettishly from the kitchen doorway, wafting a bottle-opener in her hand.

"Hey, that's my girl!"

Aaarghh! "That's my girl"? Hasn't Will the Toy-Boy noticed that Helen hasn't been a girl for *several decades*?

"Sure you don't want a glass, Jude?" Helen asks me, as Will takes charge of the tissue-wrapped bottle once again and heads towards the kitchen to join her.

"No. I'm going upstairs." I shake my head, keen to get

away from the gruesome twosome before I throw up my minimalist Christmas dinner. (It had been Japanese-themed with not a trace of reassuring stodge or custard about it.)

"Coke, then? Orange juice? Water? Oh, well, please yourself..." I hear Helen call and then grumble up the stairs after me.

I can't believe her, I really can't, I think to myself as I charge into my room and slam the door behind me. *She has the cheek to invite this Will person around for Christmas night and she hasn't even told me. It's not as if I wanted to spend time alone with her, but...*

But everything's conspiring against me at the moment – even the window has gone stiff with the cold and damp and refuses to budge. How am I meant to have a cigarette if I can't hang my head out there in the freezing night air? Mind you, why should I worry about Helen finding out my guilty secret anyway? If she can smell smoke, that's just tough – and she's probably too busy right now snogging on the sofa with *Will* to notice anyway...

"Come on..." I mumble under my breath, fumbling around in my bag for my elusive ciggies and matches. As I do that, my fingers wrap instead around my mobile, and immediately I think of all that season of goodwill blah-de-blah again. Shaunna and Molly might have put me on a ban when it comes to phoning either my dad or Gareth again till *they* call *me*, but then that's just when we're talking everyday stuff, isn't it? But this isn't every day – it's Christmas Day, and if this isn't a legitimate time to get in touch with both of them, then I don't know what is.

But which one will I try first?

Putting all thoughts of stress-smoking aside for now, I grab my phone out and flip to the address section, scrolling madly up and down till this eenie-meenie-mynie-mo process lands me on my dad's number.

Now all I can do is dial him, and hope that *she* doesn't answer…

"Hello?" says his voice, after an interminable amount of rings.

"Dad? It's me. Jude," I say, explaining myself dumbly, like he might have a lot of estranged teenage daughters calling him up tonight.

"Jude!" he hisses, instantly dropping his voice. "Hold on!"

Then there's a muffled rasping noise, as if he's put his hand over the receiver. Nevertheless, I can just make out the faint, indistinct mumble of voices: one male, one female and one of the high-pitched baby variety. There's a distant bang of a door, and two seconds later – when my dad next speaks – it's only his voice I can hear, like he's turned down the volume on the other two.

"Jude! What are you calling me for?" he says urgently, which kind of knocks me a little, if you want to know the truth.

"I just wanted to say Merry Christmas, that's all," I tell him very reasonably, not even planning on mentioning the yawning chasm of silence I've heard from him during the last three weeks.

"Jude! This is not the right time for that!" his slightly panicked voice surprises me.

What? Christmas Day is not the right time to say Merry Christmas? But a confused "Why?" is all I manage to say.

I hear Dad sigh a long, worried sigh, and some old, for-gotten memory throws up an image of him rubbing a hand through his hair. Though that must be tricky for him these days, with the amount of gel he wears in it now.

"Listen, Jude – it's difficult."

"Difficult how? What's difficult, Dad?" I ask, aware of an edge of hurt creeping into my voice.

"Well…"

He's doing that sighing thing again.

"…I haven't told Maggie that we've been in touch. It would just be too … well, too *upsetting* for her."

"Upsetting for *her*?" I squeak, not sure I'm actually hear-ing what I'm hearing.

"Well, yes! You have to understand that it's very difficult when you're the second wife—"

"The second *wife*! When did you two get married?" I demand.

I don't know why I should be so shocked to hear that – I mean, he's been with the woman for four years and has a child with her, but for God's sake, didn't he think that was the sort of detail that might be worth mentioning when we met?

"When the divorce from your mother came through, of course."

Of course? Why "of course"? Does Helen know any-thing about this? Obviously, she knew she and Dad were divorced – she'd had to sign the official papers – but does she have any inkling that Dad's gone and got himself remarried?

"And you didn't think I might want to know something like that, Dad?"

Secret babies ... secret weddings ... was there anything else he'd like to get off his chest?

"Well, that's not the important thing, Jude. What's important is nobody getting hurt, and as the second wife, you have to understand that Maggie would feel very insecure if she knew we were in touch, so it's better if we keep it as our little secret."

"You mean ... you don't *ever* plan on telling her?" I ask, disbelievingly.

"Well, no. It's for the best, you have to understand. Oh, and you haven't told your mother, have you? Because like I said to you when we met, I don't think she could handle—"

In one fluid movement, I press the end-call button and fling my phone at the nearest wall, hardly even registering as a chunk of plastic casing splinters off.

I guess that puts paid to calling Gareth next. Not that I have the energy to face any more potential disappointment tonight...

"Hey, Jude! Brilliant!" Shaunna beams as soon as she opens her front door to me. "What made you change your mind about coming over?"

"Oh, let's see... How about the fact that, on a scale of importance in their lives, both my parents rate me somewhere below the milkman and just above the slugs in the garden?" I suggest, mining some seam of black humour in my soul (which at least beats crying).

"I see," Shaunna nods, understanding more than I've said in words. "But if you come in, you have to accept that there *will* be enforced wearing of paper hats, and my parents *will* insist on you eating your body weight in custard and Christmas pudding!"

"I understand," I nod solemnly, shivering only slightly on her doorstep.

"And you won't mind that my gran is slightly tipsy on Bailey's and keeps breaking into choruses of 'Danny Boy', even though she doesn't know the words?"

"No problem."

"And are you truly, *truly* ready for playing a game of Twister with me, Adam, Ruth and Boring Brian?"

"What do you get if you win?"

"Extra helpings of Christmas pudding and custard."

"Count me in," I tell Shaunna, as she ushers me into her Christmas wonderland of family mayhem, fairy lights and the scent of pine needles.

Bliss...

chapter eighteen

Can I have some extra fun with that?

Date:	*Tuesday 31st December*
Stressometer rating:	*Medium. Got some party butter flies in my tummy.*
Wish of the moment:	*That I start the New Year as a new, improved me.*

Once upon a time there was scaredy-cat Jude, who was a world-class expert in Worrying and Fretting.

But after Christmas, scaredy-cat Jude made a marginally early New Year's resolution to dump the worrying and the fretting, and get more determined and confident instead.

So … when Helen told me (surprise, surprise) that she'd be going out on New Year's Eve to some party or other with her friends (including her *very* good friend Will, presumably), I decided to have a party of my own. In my house. And no one – not even Mr Moany Watson next door – is going to stop me.

"So, Jude," says Adam, sidling up to me in the kitchen as

I scramble around in our over-stuffed drawers for the ever-disappearing bottle-opener. "Who are all these people here tonight?"

I straighten up and gaze around the kitchen, at a sea of faces I don't recognize. It looks like Anya took me at my word when I popped round to see her a few days ago. ("Invite who you want! The more the merrier!") The same goes for the rest of the house – it's now 11.30 p.m., and the whole place, with the exception of some mates from school and some pals of Dean and Adam's – is full of party animals whom I've never met before in my life. And somehow, it makes me feel liberated and brilliant to have loads of new, potentially interesting people packing out my normally woefully under-popu-lated house.

"I don't know who they all are," I tell Adam, "but as long as they're having fun, I don't care."

Fun – that's what I want. More please.

And as long as Gareth turns up soon, all the better. I texted him earlier in the week, and presume – since he texted back to say fine, he'd try to make it – that he's going to be here soon... Anytime would suit me, just as long as I can start this next year with a kiss and the chance of happiness with a good guy for a change. I still haven't had a proper chat with him since I saw him in the alley behind the pub a week or so ago, but New Year's like a whole new beginning, isn't it? Time to forget what's in the past and look to the future...

"Hi!" Anya smiles, walking into the kitchen like a glow-ing ray of silver: silver combat trousers, silver bangles, silver ribbon twisted through her pink and purple extensions.

Only her white, platform Buffalo trainers and tight pink top add a clash of non-metallic.

"Got to take this back to Shaunna!" Adam grins at me, holding up a plastic cup before he disappears.

"Hi," I grin at Anya, once Adam bounces off in his usual enthusiastic Tigger stride.

"Having a good time?" Anya smiles, settling herself against the work surface next to me.

"Of course!" I smile, specially now I've found the bottle-opener in amongst the tea-towels.

"Good, good…" Anya nods.

That "Good, good…", that means something, I can tell. I put the bottle-opener down and stare at her.

"And?" I ask her.

"And … and I wanted to talk to you about something, Jude," Anya bats her mascara-laden eyelashes at me. "*Someone*, I mean."

"Who's that, then?"

My heart is hammering. I hate this; my heart has done so much hammering in the last few weeks that I've got internal bruising, I'm sure.

"It's, um, Gareth," she states, just as I suspected she would. "I knew already that you really liked him; I saw the two of you together at my party. But I was chatting to Shaunna just now and she was telling me that you were kind of hoping he'd be here tonight. And I thought I'd better tell you, I don't think that's going to happen."

"Why not?" I ask, feeling all the fun seep out of my soul.

"Because I know for a fact that he's arranged to go to a party with Donna."

As I let that little nugget sink in, I find Anya has more

gems up her non-existent sleeve…

"And since you still like him so much, Jude, I thought I should tell you about him and Donna."

"What *about* him and Donna?" I hear myself ask breathily.

"Well, him and Donna have this weird thing… They've been going out together for about two years, and they seem to really get off on splitting up and getting back together again. I think they really like the drama of it all – the fighting and making up."

"So, what are you saying?" I ask Anya, straight out. "They're back together *now*?"

My heart is thundering fit to burst. In fact, it's thundering along in time to the Portishead track that's now blasting from the living room. I dug out a couple of CDs from Dad's secret, left-behind stash earlier. Well, there's no point in keeping them hidden away like some priceless treasures…

"Yes, no, maybe. Who knows?" Anya shrugs her bare shoulders. "It's just that I wanted to warn you that it's not a great idea to fall for him. The problem with Gareth is – apart from never quite ending things with Donna – he can't resist … well, *vulnerable* girls. He loves playing the good guy, the understanding guy who doles out sympathy. I don't know if it makes him feel powerful or what. But when he meets someone like you, who pours out her heart, then it's perfect. Until he gets bored, of course."

I used to admire Anya, but suddenly I don't – she's as interfering as any old granny, and doesn't know what she's talking about.

"How could you possibly know that I've been 'pouring

my heart out' to Gareth?" I quiz her, thinking of all the personal conversations he and I have had about the situation with my dad.

"Because he told me," says Anya, pure and simple. "We're in a lot of the same classes at art school. And another thing... I know what you're going through with him – 'cause I've been there too."

I shut up, my resentment at her instantly on hold.

"What do you mean?"

"I *mean*," Anya explains quietly, so as not to be heard by everyone around us in the kitchen, "I got suckered in by Gareth too, just when I'd been dumped by my boyfriend. Gareth looked out for me, flattered me, sympathized with me, till I was head-over-heels, and then he backed off, like it had never happened. Then I found out that he and Donna were an item again. Nearly broke my heart. And Ben and Neil nearly broke his *neck* over that one."

"Ben and Neil?" I frown, vaguely aware that I'd seen Neil at least arrive with Anya a couple of hours earlier.

"Yeah – they hate Gareth. Can't stand him, after what he did to me, *and* a couple of other girls we all know. I know Neil can come out with stupid stuff when he's nervous or shy, but that's why he didn't exactly rush to give you Gareth's number that day when you came round to my flat..."

Oh. The business with the local Pizza Hut number. And of course that was the day Ben had made the snippy remark about me chasing after Gareth, when he thought I was out of earshot. So ... was that more a dig at Gareth than at me?

"I didn't realize..." I mumble flatly, beginning to feel

like a fool (yet again). God … I thought I'd got myself a good guy when all the time, he was just a bad boy in disguise. A wolf in hamster's clothing…

"And then of course, there's the fact that Neil really, really likes –"

I want to keep listening to what Anya's saying, but two things are stopping me. First: I'm struggling as it is to take on board the information she's just given me and I'm not sure I can handle any more. Secondly: the doorbell is ringing incessantly, and no one is bothering to answer it.

"Sorry," I apologize to Anya. "Back in a minute…"

I squeeze past a bundle of roaring, arguing people in the hallway (the reason, I think, that no one apart from specially-attuned me seems to be able to hear the doorbell), and pull the front door open. And you know something? I know I'm an airhead, but I *still* find myself hoping – despite what Anya's just told me – that it's going to be Gareth, armed with believable excuses for not phoning me.

Instead, it's Mr Watson, in his dressing gown and complaining about the noise. Which at least this time *is* my responsibility.

"This music!" he booms at me.

"It's Portishead," I announce. "Do you like it? I could make a tape of it for you if you want…"

In the face of my disrespectful, bare-faced teenaged cheek, Mr Watson tuts loudly and mutters something about wiping the smile off my face.

He doesn't have to worry – what Anya's just told me has put paid to any more smiles tonight…

* * *

Mr Watson – what a guy. Who'd have thought he'd get some more in-house entertainment arranged for me, by calling the police?

Of course, things in the last half-hour haven't livened up just with the arrival of the local constabulary (after a certain person's complaint about the noise). Oh no. Whoever decided to fill the bath with cold water to keep the beer cool in was a person of great imagination but not a lot of patience: they put the bath plug in, turned on the cold tap, then got distracted by something or other (or just got plain bored) and shot off, leaving the bath to flood and leak horribly down the stairs and through the roof into the living room.

And the person who lit every candle in our living room was perhaps going for ambience, but hadn't accounted for people bumbling around dancing and knocking into things, and so we nearly had our own bonfire in there (luckily, water trickling down from the swamped bathroom above put out the flames trying to lick at the wallpaper). And then, when the roaring conversation in the hallway turned into a full-scale, flying fist-a-thon that stumbled into the front garden, well, Mr Watson and his binoculars had a field day...

And now? Well, now I'm hiding out in the back garden, sitting on the bench and having a cigarette, staring out into the icy darkness of Westburn Park and wondering if there's the remotest possibility of getting a break ever...

"Can I sit down?" says a soft voice.

I can't even look round, never mind acknowledge my mother. I shrug instead, and feel my insides curl up in embarrassment. Good grief; I must surely be the record-holder when it comes to having the most mortifyingly awful New Year's Eve party ever…

"The police called me."

Helen doesn't need to tell me that; I was in the hallway when they contacted her on her mobile twenty minutes ago.

"Sorry to spoil your evening," I mumble, holding my cigarette low in the vain hope that she *won't* spot it and have something else to flip out at me about.

"You didn't spoil it," says Helen. "Anyway, the way the police were talking, I thought it was going to be a *lot* worse. But it's not a big deal."

"I think my friends have tidied things up a bit," I murmur unhappily, thinking guiltily of Molly and Shaunna, Dean and Adam shooing people out while scurrying around with mops and buckets and brushes and pans – all stuff I should have been helping out with if I hadn't sneaked out here in the dark.

"Can I get a puff?" she asks.

"A puff of what?" I ask in a panic.

"Oh, come on – stop trying to hide it. Your cigarette, I mean."

"But you don't smoke!"

"Neither do you – I thought! Anyway, I know it's disgusting. I only smoke when I'm stressed…"

"Me too," I tell her in surprise.

We sit in silence for a second, both absorbing our matching secret vice.

"I spoke to Molly inside," I hear Helen say. "She told me you've been in touch with your dad quite a lot recently. That must have been fun for you. *Not.*"

I'm momentarily stumped at Helen doing teen-speak, so I say nothing.

"Listen, I know we haven't spoken properly about your dad and everything," she continues in the near-dark, "*and* that stuff about him and his girlfriend having a baby, but—"

"Wife," I correct.

"Wife? He got married again? Ha, ha! *Typical!*"

Um, I think it's fair to say that I didn't expect Helen's reaction to be a *laugh*. What was Dad saying about her not being able to handle the news?

"Oh, Jude…" she says, regaining her composure again. "He let you down, didn't he? Lots of promises, and then a big, fat nothing."

"I guess," I mumble, realizing that Molly's told her everything.

"Well, join the club, Jude. I got suckered by all his promises for years, and look where it got me."

I turn round and face her, looking at the silhouette of her face and the tiny sparkle of diamanté on her nose.

"He was just such a charmer, Jude," she continues, "always winding people around his finger and then going and doing exactly what he wanted: under all the sweet-talk, he was just a selfish git who thought only about number one. Honestly, it went on like that all through our marriage; he'd blow hot and cold till I never knew where I was with him. He even promised that we'd all go on some big holiday abroad – Australia for a month, maybe – but it must have been just guilt talking, 'cause he packed his bags and left us for that woman two weeks later. Oh, God, I'm sorry, Jude. Am I upsetting you?"

But she's mistaken my shaking shoulders for crying

when really I'm laughing. All those years I've been a mug for bad boys? Falling flat on my face in love with losers and charmers? It's not *my* fault – definitely not. I'm only following in the family tradition…

"Helen…?" I begin, a question suddenly shoving itself to the front of my brain.

"What?" she asks, gazing hard at me.

"Why didn't you want to talk about that stuff with Dad? Why didn't you ask me more about seeing him, or tell me what you've just told me now?"

"Well … after you flipped out at me that Saturday morning, I decided that I should just shut up and give you a chance to open up to me about it – but only if you were up for it. He's *your* dad – *you* had to decide for yourself how you felt about him. I didn't want to interfere with that."

"I thought you just weren't interested…"

"No way, Jude!" she splutters. "Absolutely not! In fact, the way I saw it, ever since your dad left, I've always tried to bring you up like a friend, instead of a daughter, with lots of freedom. So, I just thought, if you wanted to talk to me more about that – or anything else – fine. If you didn't, then I didn't have the right to ask."

Omigod. All these years I thought my mother didn't care; instead, she was trying to raise me using some alternative, hippy-dippy method of child-rearing. Pity she didn't let me in on the secret – I could have enjoyed the experience a whole lot more.

"Look – it's bloody freezing out here," says Helen, her teeth beginning to chatter. "What about we go in? I left Will giving your mates a hand tidying the place up. Maybe if we're lucky, there'll be nothing left for us to do!"

"Maybe," I find myself smiling, as I stand up on cold-stiffened legs and start following her inside. "So, Helen…"

"What?" she turns, looking serious, maybe expecting more questions about Dad. (But I'm too tired for more of *those* till later.)

"This Will. He's not like my dad, then?" I find myself asking her.

"No – Will's one of the good guys," Helen laughs.

"Guys? Don't you mean *boys*? Isn't he about twelve?" I giggle, a trickle of that black humour showing through. I think I'm mildly hysterical, all things considered.

"He's only a little bit younger than me, Jude," Helen surprises me by saying. "He's 30 and he's a mature student, like me."

Wow – I'd never reckoned that he was that age, but then plenty of things are surprising me tonight.

"Oh, and hey – what about we make a New Year's Resolution together, Jude?" Helen says, as we walk up the path together.

"What?" I ask, bemused.

"We give up cigarettes? Even when we're stressed?"

"OK." I smile, even though she can't see it on my face.

Well … me and Helen. It's going to take a long time till we get used to trusting each other, I guess, but a pathetic habit of falling for losers and a determination to give up smoking in common is a pretty good place to start…

The house is mostly empty and quiet now, apart from the murmur of my friends' voices and the rustle of rubbish bags being filled.

"Molly? Shaun?" I ask, hearing the tinkle of a dustpan and brush scooping up something broken and glassy in the living room.

But it's not Molly, *or* Shaunna, *or* Dean or Adam, for that matter. It's not even Will the not-so Toy-Boy, who I've just passed rustling up a vat of tea for everyone in the kitchen, with a little help from Helen.

"Oh, hi," says Neil, from his crouched position by the fireplace.

I'm surprised by three things: 1) that he's here at all, since Anya and all of his other art school buddies are long gone; 2) that he's on his hands and knees cleaning my house; and 3) that he doesn't look nearly so trendy with a blue plastic dustpan and brush in his hands.

Oh, and I forgot the most surprising thing ... he can smile.

"Thought I'd stick around and give you a hand tidying this mess up," he shrugs, revealing teeth and dimples I've never seen before.

"That's, um, nice of you," I reply, feeling slightly confused. But then this whole night's been a jumble of confusion, so what's new?

"Right, that's *that* done," he states, straightening up and holding out the dustpan with the remnants of a wine glass in it. "Course, you'll need something to get that red wine out of the carpet..."

It's pretty funny seeing this tall, lean guy who could be an extra member of Travis or the Stereophonics or something standing there chattering about stain removal.

"Maybe we'll have something in the cupboard," I hear myself saying, although I doubt that very much, knowing that our cupboards hold many things, but most of them are useless.

Then there's this odd moment where we gaze at each other, shyly smiling and not knowing what to say next. I don't know what's going through Neil's mind, but all I can think is, *What's he* doing *here?* And then I vaguely remember the tail-end of what Anya was telling me. What was it again? Something along the lines of… "And then of course, there's the fact that Neil really, really likes…"

A jangle from my back pocket breaks the awkward silence and I nervously mumble something in Neil's direction about a text message as I reach for my mobile.

"Jude – sorry can't make yr party. Meet tomorrow? Noon? By town hall? Luv Gareth x."

"Somebody wishing you Happy New Year?" Neil asks, as Big Ben starts *bong*ing on the telly that I hadn't even noticed was switched on. From the kitchen, I can hear Helen yelling out "Happy New Year, everybody!" and the voices of my friends cheering from various points around the house.

"Something like that," I reply to Neil's question, while I stare at the message.

Is it really from Gareth? Or is it another wind-up courtesy of the delightful Donna and her cronies? Either way, it doesn't really matter. Quickly, I key in my reply and press send: "*Get lost.*" There, that should do it.

"Maybe we should…?"

Neil is pointing his brush in the direction of the laughter and whooping coming from the kitchen where it sounds like our miniaturized party is congregating, as the bongs from Big Ben keep bonging.

"Yeah, I guess we should." I shrug, and start to make a move when I clatter awkwardly into Neil, who is trying to step past me, dustpan outstretched so he doesn't spill any shards of glass.

"Well, Happy New Year, Jude!" he laughs, gazing down at me, his smile only centimetres from my face.

Neil... What a revelation, in a night of revelations. Behind the fancy dress of looking too aloof and trendy for his own good is a kind boy who sweeps, smiles and finds the patience to stick around for me when I've been busy hankering after entirely the wrong lad. 'Cause I may only have a peanut for a brain, but I think I can work out the end of Anya's sentence, and it *does* seem that Neil really, *really* likes me, from the way he is softly kissing me now...

"Hey, Jude! Where are you?" I hear Shaunna calling out.

I'm right here, and Shaunna and everyone else can wait a few minutes longer to give me their New Year's hugs and kisses, since I'm otherwise occupied with Neil.

You know, I've got a talent for getting instant monster crushes on people, but I've never done it this way round before – fallen for a good guy who was *disguised* as a bad boy, I mean. And I've never been kissed by anyone who's holding a blue plastic dustpan and brush either.

But hey, it's New Year, and anything can happen, right...?

KaReN MᶜComBie

"A funny and talented author."
Books Magazine

Once upon a time (OK, 1990), Karen McCombie
jumped in her beat-up car with her boyfriend and
a very bad-tempered cat, leaving her native Scotland behind for
the bright lights of London and a desk at "J17" magazine.
She's lived in London and acted like a teenager ever since.

The fiction bug bit after writing short stories for "Sugar"
magazine. Next came a flurry of teen novels, and of course
the best-selling "Ally's World" series, set around and named
after Alexandra Palace in North London, close to where
Karen lives with her husband Tom, little daughter Milly
and an assortment of cats.

PS. If you want to know more about Karen check out her
website at karenmccombie.com. Karen says,
"It's sheeny and shiny, furry and, er funny (in places)!
It's everything you could want from a website and a weeny
bit more..."

**Want to know more about
Shaunna, Jude and Molly?**

Then don't miss:

my Funny
Valentine

Shaunna isn't fussy – much. She's just not going to settle for an ordinary guy, like her sister's gone and done. Ruth's got this cutesy white wedding planned, but Shaunna can't imagine anything more cringey…

Stuff red roses and corny romance – Shaunna wants a sweet soulmate who'll drape daisy chains around her neck. But is the boy of her daydreams out there anywhere?